I'M WATCHING YOU...

"Who is this?" Julia asks the voice on the phone.

"Just wanted you to know I can see everything you do."

A crash in the dining room sends Julia's heart into her throat. The window is broken. Glass glitters on the wood floor. A round package lies next to a potted plant in the corner. It's a rock wrapped in paper and tied with a string.

Julia takes the paper from the rock and looks at it.

Written on an old typewriter are two words that set her heart thundering: "YOU'RE NEXT!"

Other Avon Flare Books by
Carol Gorman

DIE FOR ME
GRAVEYARD MOON

Avon Books are available at special quantity discounts for bulk purchases for sales promotions, premiums, fund raising or educational use. Special books, or book excerpts, can also be created to fit specific needs.

For details write or telephone the office of the Director of Special Markets, Avon Books, Dept. FP, 1350 Avenue of the Americas, New York, New York 10019, 1-800-238-0658.

BACK FROM THE DEAD

CAROL GORMAN

If you purchased this book without a cover, you should be aware that this book is stolen property. It was reported as "unsold and destroyed" to the publisher, and neither the author nor the publisher has received any payment for this "stripped book."

BACK FROM THE DEAD is an original publication of Avon Books. This work has never before appeared in book form. This work is a novel. Any similarity to actual persons or events is purely coincidental.

AVON BOOKS
A division of
The Hearst Corporation
1350 Avenue of the Americas
New York, New York 10019

Copyright © 1995 by Carol Gorman
Published by arrangement with the author
Library of Congress Catalog Card Number: 95-94312
ISBN: 0-380-77433-X
RL: 5.6

All rights reserved, which includes the right to reproduce this book or portions thereof in any form whatsoever except as provided by the U.S. Copyright Law. For information address Writers House, Inc., 21 West 26th Street, New York, New York 10010.

First Avon Flare Printing: November 1995

AVON FLARE TRADEMARK REG. U.S. PAT. OFF. AND IN OTHER COUNTRIES, MARCA REGISTRADA, HECHO EN U.S.A.

Printed in the U.S.A.

RA   10   9   8   7   6   5   4   3   2   1

To my friend, Rob Nassif,
who writes beautiful music
and makes a mean cup of herbal tea

1

It was nearly dark as we climbed into the hills that night. Nikki had said we were there "looking for adventure," but I couldn't imagine what kind of adventure we'd find. Five of the six of us were plastered.

I had no idea that before the night was over, somebody would be dead.

I didn't want to be here any more than Nikki wanted me. She and I had barely spoken since we'd left the house to pick up the others.

She and Matt led the way, stumbling through the brush and tangled weeds. They each carried a can of beer in one hand and a six-pack in the other. We all had backpacks stuffed with fireplace logs and blankets.

"Look at the moon!" Nikki said, gazing at the huge orange orb hanging in the eastern sky.

Matt threw back his head and howled, and the others laughed and howled with him.

Nikki took a drink from her beer can. "I've heard that people get crazy under a full moon. More murders are committed during that time than any other."

"Maybe there's a murderer in these hills," said Randy Shaw. "He'll find our campfire and bludgeon us all to death."

"Or one of us will go insane and kill the rest, and all that'll be left is a bloody mass of bones, hair, and denim," said Matt.

"Shut up." Nikki turned to me, smirking. "We don't want to scare poor Julia."

They all looked back at me and sneered, including Sean Wallace, my so-called date, who was more drunk than anyone. Nikki had picked Sean especially for me tonight.

Bless her heart.

Nikki Stott hates me. I'm not too crazy about her, either, even though she's my cousin. I'd moved in with her family just before school had started two weeks earlier. Mom and Dad needed some time alone, they'd said, to work on saving their marriage. They'd promised it would be just for one semester.

This morning I'd heard Nikki arguing with her mother about me. "Why do I have to drag her with me every place I go? I didn't ask her to come here and wreck my life. She doesn't fit in. All she cares about are her grades and being perfect. I'm sick of her!"

"She's my sister's only child," my Aunt Helen had said. "I owe it to her to help. I'm sure Julia's upset about the trouble her parents are having, and she doesn't know anyone else in Franklin Heights. She must feel lonely, so you should include her when you go out with your friends."

"Poor Julia," Nikki had said, her voice filled with contempt.

Aunt Helen had sighed. She didn't understand that I didn't *want* to be a part of Nikki's social life. I had nothing in common with Nikki or her friends. In fact, most of the time, they either bored or exasperated me. All they thought about were their parties and beer. And football. Matt, Sean, and Randy were heroes in town because they were on the football team.

There wasn't much else to do in Franklin Heights for entertainment.

"This is the perfect place for a mass murder," Matt said. "Lonely and deserted."

Sean laughed. "No one would hear the screams."

"It'd be cool if it happened to somebody else," Nikki said, grinning slyly. "We'd read about it in the paper and try to figure out who the murderer was."

I'd been so stupid to let Aunt Helen talk me into going with them. I *knew* it would be like this.

A movement in the brush about twenty yards to our right caught my attention.

"What's that?" I said.

"What?" Sean said, loping along at my side. "I don't see anything."

I could've pointed out that he was in no condition to see an elephant stampede right in front of him but decided Sean might not care for my sarcasm.

A face peered out of the deepening shadows. A guy.

Brandi shrieked.

He scrambled out of his hiding place and ran into the moonlight. He paused a second and stared at us. He had a dirty face and wore clothes that were soiled and torn. His mouth hung open.

Matt picked up a stone and threw it at the man. "Get out of here, man! You're crashing our party!"

"Cut it out, Matt," I said. "Leave him alone."

The man scurried across the clearing and tripped at the far end where the woods began. He scrambled to his feet and disappeared into the woods.

Sean laughed. "Look at him go!"

"And don't come back!" yelled Nikki.

"What a spooky guy," said Brandi. "I bet he was a hobo. Maybe he jumped off a train at the bottom of the hill."

"Have you ever seen anyone so dirty and ugly?" Nikki said. "He couldn't have been much older than us."

"Maybe he's a mass murderer," Randy said.

"Julia didn't like it when you threw that rock," Brandi said to Matt.

"Well, you know where Julia can go." Matt mumbled it, but I heard what he'd said.

"She can go wherever she wants to go," Nikki said. "Just so it's out of my life."

"Okay, look," I said. "Why don't you guys just take me back to town?"

"Oh, right," Nikki said. "And you'll tell my mom we dumped you! Forget it."

"Drop me off at the library," I said. "I'll read till they close and then walk over to the Doughnut

Palace. You can pick me up there later."

"I'm not driving you clear back to town!" Nikki said. "So just quit whining."

Sean laughed. "That's good." He looked at me unsteadily and peered closely into my face. "Quit whining, woman."

His beer breath turned my stomach. Yechk.

"Terrific," I said, turning my head away from Sean.

"Come on, let's go," Nikki said. She started off into the clearing.

We followed her to where the man had vanished.

"We have to walk through the woods to get higher into the hills," Matt said. He pulled out a flashlight. "I'll lead the way."

We followed Matt into the woods. It was very dark, and I wished I'd thought to bring a flashlight. If Sean had been sober, I could have held onto his arm. But he was more likely to fall than anyone else, and I didn't want him to take me down, too. He was a linebacker, six-three, and probably over two hundred pounds; I'd get squashed if he fell on top of me.

"Isn't there a path we could follow?" Nikki asked.

"We're following it," Matt said. "It's hard to see." He shone the flashlight on a faint path at his feet.

A couple of times a small animal scrambled through the underbrush to get out of our way, and each time Nikki screamed and grabbed Matt's arm.

"Relax, will you?" Matt said. "It's just a rabbit or something."

It took about twenty minutes to make our way through the woods and into a clearing. Coming out of the darkness among the trees, the clearing appeared bright and silvery under the moonlight.

A figure was crossing the clearing ahead.

"Hey, there's the hobo again," Brandi said, pointing.

"No," Nikki said. "The hobo was wearing dark clothes, and this guy's wearing a light-colored jacket."

"Man, this place is becoming Grand Central Station," Matt said. "I thought these hills were deserted."

"Hey, isn't he that weird kid at school?" Brandi said, peering into the distance.

"Yeah!" Randy said. "Look at him limp. That's Heath Quinn."

"It *is* Quinn!" Nikki said. "He's got on that ratty, beige jacket he always wears."

I knew who Heath was. He was in my lit class. He sat in the back of the room and had only spoken during one discussion.

We'd been assigned to read Poe's "The Cask of Amontillado" in the first week of school. Most of the students hadn't done their homework, so the half-dozen or so people who had read it did most of the talking.

"I think Poe should have said what this Fortunato guy did to deserve getting buried alive inside the brick wall," said April Briar. "I didn't know whether to feel sorry for him or not."

"Does it matter?" asked Ms. Cater, our teacher. "Should Fortunato have to die this hideous death because he had made Montresor angry?"

April shrugged.

Ms. Cater looked down at the list of student names on a sheet of paper. "Matt?"

Matt slid down in his seat and folded his arms. "I dunno."

"Did you read the story?"

"No." He looked around the room, grinning.

Most of the kids—especially the ones who also hadn't read it—snickered.

"Well, how do you feel about revenge?" Ms. Cater asked.

Matt continued grinning. "I believe in it."

More snickers.

"I think April's right," a blonde said from across the room. "It depends on what the person did to you."

"Why do you think the viewpoint character doesn't tell us what Fortunato had done to him?" Ms. Cater asked. She looked down at her student list, then up at me. "Julia?"

"Maybe it wasn't important," I said. "Maybe we're supposed to wonder about revenge in general and not about whether Fortunato deserved to die."

"Do you think most people believe in revenge?" Ms. Cater asked. "Heath?"

Her question was met with silence.

I turned back to look for the student named Heath.

A guy with greasy, dark hair slicked straight back gazed up from his desk. I saw something in his eyes that set off alarms in my head. He looked *haunted*.

"Heath?" Ms. Cater repeated.

He stared at the far wall, not at Ms. Cater.

"Everyone believes in revenge," he said. His voice was soft and without expression.

"Everyone?"

"It makes the world go 'round."

Eve Lenhart, who sits next to me, turned to face him. "I thought it was love that makes the world go 'round," she said.

"No," Heath said. "Hate and revenge are the most powerful forces in the universe."

There were more snickers, but this time the laughter was directed *at* Heath.

"What a dweeb," Matt said, snickering.

The discussion continued, but I couldn't get my mind off that dark-haired guy in the back with the haunted eyes. I wondered about his pain and his anger, and I wanted to know more about him.

I wished I could turn and look at him again, but I didn't.

That was the only time he'd spoken in two weeks.

"Hey," Nikki said now, "let's follow him! I want to see where he's going."

"Yeah," Matt said. "What's he doing up here, anyway?"

"Looks like he knows where he's going," Brandi said. "Even limping, he's going pretty fast."

"Don't get too close," Matt said. "I bet he doesn't even know we're here."

"We'll sneak up on him," Randy said. He imitated Heath's walk, and the others laughed and limped, too.

We headed toward Heath and followed him at a distance.

"We can't get too far behind or we'll lose him," Nikki said. "I want to see where he goes."

Seconds after she'd said it, Heath disappeared into a stand of trees.

"I *told* you not to get too far behind!" Nikki said.

"Let's keep going," Matt said. "We'll catch up."

We walked to the trees and stopped.

"Hey, look, there's another path!" Brandi said.

We followed the path through the trees and climbed higher and higher, past rocky outcroppings and more woods. We glimpsed Heath ahead of us as he reached the far edge of the trees on top of the hill.

Heath had to have known we were following him by then. Nikki, Matt, and Brandi were talking in loud voices about him as if he couldn't hear us.

"He's so gross!" Nikki said.

"He hardly ever says a word to anyone," Brandi said.

"He lives with his mom and dad in a crappy house at the edge of town. His dad's drunk all the time," Matt said.

At the top of the hill, we followed Heath into a clearing. There, squatting among the weeds, was a small, dilapidated cabin. Heath climbed the wooden stairs onto the sagging porch, pushed open the door, and disappeared inside.

I stared at the little building. I suppose I felt a kind of bond with Heath since he didn't fit in with these people any more than I did. Why had he come up here?

"Hey, Heath!" Matt yelled. "Come on out! We're having a party!"

"We've got lots of beer!" Nikki hollered. "The more the merrier!" She laughed and Brandi giggled, too.

There was no response or movement at the door or windows.

"I don't think he wants to come out and play," Sean said, pretending to be disappointed.

"Come on, let's go find a spot for a campfire," I said.

"I think *this* is a good spot for a campfire," Sean said.

Matt laughed. "Yeah, he'll come out for sure if we set a campfire on his front porch!"

Nikki grinned. "It'll scare him to death!"

They began unpacking their backpacks, taking out the logs and gathering up brush on the ground.

"Are you *kidding?*" I said. I couldn't imagine that they were serious. "You aren't really going to set a fire on the porch, are you?"

"Shut up, Julia," Nikki said. "You ruin everything."

"You can't do that!" I said.

"Just watch us," Matt said. He piled the wood on the porch and stuffed some newspapers under it.

I ran onto the porch and kicked at the logs, shoving them off the porch. "You jerks," I screamed.

"You're all drunk! Stop it! Heath!" I yelled. "They're starting a fire on the porch! You'd better come out!"

Nikki bounded up the steps and smacked me across the mouth. "I said, shut up!"

White lights flashed across my eyes. I shoved Nikki hard to the side and banged on the door.

"Heath!" I yelled again. "Come out! They're going to set fire to this place."

Matt grabbed me and threw me off the porch. I fell backward on my butt in the weeds.

Matt took out a lighter and set fire to the newspapers under the logs.

"Heath!" I shouted. *"Heath!"*

Still there was no response from inside the house.

Flames leaped up from the logs, crackling and popping. A lick of fire crept along the edge of the brittle wooden porch. Flames jumped higher and set the porch roof on fire.

Nikki and Matt whooped.

"Heath!" I yelled. "*Please* come out!"

"Would you look at that place go!" Sean said, grinning.

"Too bad Heath won't join our party," Randy said.

"Just watch," Matt said. "He'll come running out here any second."

"And if you think he *walks* funny," Nikki said, "wait till you see him run!" Everyone laughed.

Matt held up a beer can. "To you, Heath! I dedicate this party in your honor!"

The others raised their cans and echoed. "To Heath!"

Now the entire cabin was engulfed in fire. Heavy smoke heaved upward into the night air.

There was a long moment before anyone spoke.

"Why isn't he coming out, Matt?" Nikki said. She pushed a strand of hair out of her face.

"How should I know?" Matt said.

"Maybe he's hurt," I said, "and he can't get out."

"You wanna rescue him, Julia?" Nikki said. "Go get him. We won't stop you."

By now, though, that was impossible. The front door was burning wildly, as was the whole front wall of the cabin.

I ran around to the back. There was no door. There were two screenless windows; one was open about six inches, but too high for me to reach.

"Heath!" I screamed. "Heath! Can you hear me? You can get out through the back window!"

The only response was a lick of fire that whipped out the window above me.

"Heath!"

I ran around to the front of the cabin.

Nikki, Matt, Brandi, Randy, and Sean sat in silence, watching the inferno before them. They had to be thinking what I was thinking—there was no way Heath Quinn could survive this fire.

The heat of the blaze was unbearable.

"Let's get out of here," Nikki said.

One of the side walls gave way, and the entire roof of the cabin collapsed in on itself.

Nikki cried out and buried her face in her hands. "I want to go home."

"He's dead," Brandi said. "Heath's dead."

"Don't say that!" Nikki cried.

"Why not?" I said. "It's the truth."

"Shut up, Julia!" Nikki screamed. "Don't ever say that again!"

"Let's get out of here," Matt said. "But first, pick up *everything* we brought. Don't leave any evidence that we were here!"

2

"I swear, if you tell anybody, Julia, I'll say it was your idea. And everybody will back me up. You know they will."

Nikki sat on her bed. She clutched her pillow over her stomach and glowered at me.

We'd arrived home a few minutes ago. Aunt Helen and Uncle Jim had just disappeared into their bedroom for the night. We'd managed a curt *yes* to Aunt Helen's question, as to whether we had a good time.

Then I'd followed Nikki to her bedroom.

"Nikki, a guy was killed tonight. Doesn't that mean anything to you?"

"We don't know he was killed!" she said. "Maybe he escaped somehow. Maybe he got out the back way."

"That's possible, but I don't think so. The cabin was sitting in a clearing. We would've seen him if he'd run in any direction. Except maybe straight back. But it's probably a half mile to the trees. He didn't have time to run that far."

"We still don't know that he died!" Nikki said. "We don't know anything!"

"Chances are very good that Heath was killed, and the fire caused his death. You know that."

"Get out of my room," Nikki said. "I don't want to talk about this anymore."

"We *have* to talk about it! You can't pretend it didn't happen! This was *murder*!"

"I hate you, Julia! You've ruined my life."

"*I*'ve ruined your life?"

"Why did you have to come here!" Nikki cried. "Everything was fine until you showed up!"

"Nikki—"

"Get out of my room and keep your mouth shut about Heath Quinn. You'll be up to your neck in trouble if you tell. I'll make sure of that!"

I knew she meant it. She wasn't going to change her mind about going to the sheriff. She and her friends would stick together, keep quiet, and never tell what happened.

And if I went to the sheriff, all five of them would say it was my idea to set fire to the cabin.

We had a conspiracy of silence.

To hide a murder.

I hurried down the hall from chemistry on Monday morning and arrived early to my lit class.

Heath wasn't there, of course. I knew he wouldn't be, but I'd hoped that he'd miraculously survived that awful fire. Maybe he'd surprise me and come and sit silently in the back of the room as always.

But the period wore on, and Heath still didn't show up. I glanced at Matt a couple of times. He wasn't wearing his usual sneer, and he didn't offer any stupid comments in the class discussion.

He wouldn't look at me, either. I guess Matt actually had a conscience.

I hoped it would eat him alive.

My conscience was working hard on me, too. Heath was dead—he *must* be dead. And I'd been with the people who had killed him.

Why hadn't I fought harder? Why hadn't I *made* Nikki and her friends put out the fire? I'd tried but failed. If only I'd fought harder. Maybe I could have saved Heath's life. I was as guilty as they were.

My chest ached, and I couldn't pay attention to what Ms. Cater was saying. And I didn't care.

I stood up mechanically at the end of class and moved toward the door. I felt a touch on my arm and looked up to see Eve Lenhart.

"Julia," she said, "I'm a feature reporter for *The Bugle*. Some of our best writers graduated last year, and we need at least one new reporter. Would you be interested in joining the staff?"

I wasn't in the mood to think about writing for the school paper. I couldn't even concentrate on my class work right now. All I could think about was Heath. And all I could feel right now was guilt.

But I didn't have any friends here, and Eve seemed to be a nice person. Maybe I'd have more in common with her than the other people I'd met at school so far. I couldn't tell her what had happened to Heath, but I needed someone in Franklin Heights I could talk to.

I stopped and turned to her. "I've never written newspaper articles," I said.

"I hadn't either until I joined *The Bugle* staff last year. It's a family tradition. My brother Rick was the editor when he was a senior."

Eve smiled at me, and her pale blue eyes crinkled at the edges. She was pretty in an ordinary way. Her blond hair was shoulder-length and turned under at the ends, and her thinness gave her a fragile, doll-like quality.

"Why don't you come to the meeting after school on Wednesday?" she said.

I didn't want to. I didn't want to think about anything right now. But when she smiled, I felt I'd found a friend.

I needed her friendship.

"Okay," I said.

I wondered if Heath would appear by then. I'd feel so relieved, so *grateful* if he'd just walk through the door into my lit class tomorrow. My world would be set right again, and I would only have to get through the semester so I could go back home where I belonged.

"Good!" she said. We walked to the classroom door. "I'll tell Colin you're coming."

"Who's Colin?"

"Colin Maitland. He's a senior and *The Bugle* editor." She grinned. "You'll like him."

"Okay," I said.

"We meet in 204, the journalism room."

I smiled and nodded.

"But I'll see you in class tomorrow."

"Right," I said. "See you."

* * *

"Hope you like macaroni and cheese, Julia," Aunt Helen said.

She set the steaming casserole on the table in the breakfast nook. In the two weeks that I'd been here, we'd never eaten in the dining room. Supper was always eaten at the kitchen table in front of the TV. If we happened to be eating while *Jeopardy!* was on, we'd watch that. If we ate later, we'd watch the news.

"Sure," I said. "I like it fine."

I didn't mention that we'd had macaroni and cheese for lunch.

Nikki rolled her eyes. "We just had this crap at school."

Uncle Jim glared at Nikki. "Watch how you talk to your mother," he said.

Nikki expelled a breath of air, showing her disgust.

"Switch on the news, will you, Helen?" Uncle Jim said. "It's just starting."

My aunt turned on the set and the logo for the local channel eight news team flashed on the screen while a jingle played in the background. An announcer said, "The KBAN six o'clock evening news with anchors Jeff Saylor and Madeline Jenkins."

The two anchors sat at their news desk facing the camera. "Good evening," Jeff Saylor said. The camera moved to a close-up of him. "Headlining tonight's news, Mann County authorities are investigating the charred remains of a body found in a burned cabin ten miles north of Franklin Heights."

Nikki dropped her fork and blinked at the TV.

Uncle Jim and Aunt Helen turned their full attention to the screen.

Jeff Saylor continued. "County fire officials suspect arson in the blaze that destroyed the cabin early Sunday morning. We go now to Mandy Richards, who reports live from the scene. Mandy?"

An attractive, dark-haired woman holding a microphone stood in front of the cabin—or what was left of it. I had no doubt that it was the cabin that Matt and the others had set fire to on Saturday night. I recognized the large stones that had stood around the foundation.

Nothing was left but rubble.

"Jeff," Mandy Richards said, "as you said, the fire was discovered in the early morning hours on Sunday, but by the time fire fighters arrived at the cabin in the hilly area north of town, the cabin had burned to the ground.

"The body was found Sunday by investigators from the Mann County Fire Department. They didn't release any information about their discovery until early this morning."

The next camera shot had Jeff sitting at his anchor's desk, looking at Mandy on a large TV monitor.

"Mandy," Jeff Saylor said, "do authorities know yet the age or the sex of the person whose body was found?"

"That information isn't available yet, Jeff," she said. "An autopsy is scheduled for tomorrow, and we'll report the findings as soon as they're announced."

"Any word on who owned the cabin?" Jeff asked.

"The land and the cabin were owned by a David Swisher, who lives in Lansing. He told me this afternoon that he built the cabin for hunting about twenty years ago, but hasn't used it for several years."

"Did he have any idea who could have been killed in that fire?" Jeff asked her.

"No, Jeff," Mandy said. "As far as he knew, no one ever used the cabin."

"Thanks, Mandy," Jeff said. "We'll be waiting to hear more from you on this story."

Mandy nodded and her picture disappeared from the screen. Jeff turned to Madeline Jenkins. "Certainly a shocking discovery," he said.

"Yes, it is," Madeline said. "We'll be following this story closely."

They went on to report more news.

I looked over at Nikki. She sat rigidly in her chair, her face drained of color, her eyes big and scared.

Was she surprised? I wondered. Had she thought that no one would discover the fire at the cabin? Or Heath's body?

"Who would've set fire to a cabin with someone inside?" said Uncle Jim.

"It's so sad," Aunt Helen said.

"Maybe he was up there hunting," Uncle Jim said. "And had an argument with another hunter who decided to kill him."

"Aren't you going to eat, Nikki?" Aunt Helen said.

Nikki gazed at her mother, fear still glazing her eyes. "I'm not hungry."

"Eat a little bit," her mother said.

"I don't want any," she said, her voice rising in pitch. "I told you, we had this for lunch."

She pushed her chair away from the table and ran out of the room. Her footsteps echoed up the stairs.

Aunt Helen and Uncle Jim looked at me.

"What's with Nikki?" Uncle Jim said.

"I don't know," I said.

"I didn't realize she hated macaroni and cheese so much," Aunt Helen murmured.

"I'll go and talk to her," I said.

I excused myself and hurried up the stairs. I found Nikki lying on her back in bed, staring at the ceiling.

"You want to talk to the sheriff now?" I asked her.

She sat up on her bed. "Are you *kidding?*" she said. "And get sent to prison for the rest of my life?"

"They're going to find out," I said. "They're already investigating."

"They won't find out unless you tell," she said.

"They could find witnesses," I said. "What about that hobo in the hills? He could identify us."

"They might be able to prove we were in the hills," Nikki said. "They can't prove we set the fire."

"What if the hobo was hiding in the trees when the fire was set?" I said. "He was going up into the hills, just as we were."

21

"Stop it!" Nikki cried. "You're just trying to scare me! Get out!"

She picked up her pillow and threw it at me.

"Get out of my room. And don't tell anyone or I just might kill *you!*"

3

I switched on the news again at ten o'clock and sat on the couch to watch. Uncle Jim and Aunt Helen were sipping tea and watching TV in the kitchen, and Nikki hadn't come out of her bedroom all evening, so I had the living room to myself.

The "body in the cabin" story was again the lead item of the program. They rehashed the same information they'd reported at six o'clock, but there was nothing new on the case.

The news team went on to other stories.

A sound over my shoulder drew my attention.

I looked up to see Nikki sitting on the steps leading to the second floor, peering at the TV through the rails in the banister.

"Hey," I said.

She got up without speaking and disappeared up the stairs.

"Nikki?"

No response.

Her bedroom door slammed shut.

Heath didn't show up at school the next day or Wednesday, either.

"Anybody know where Heath is?" Ms. Cater asked. "He's not been at school for three days, but he hasn't been excused for illness."

A few shoulders shrugged, but nobody spoke.

"Well, if anyone sees him, please tell him he should call the attendance office. Or better yet, come back to school."

I glanced at Matt. He sat still in his seat, staring at the top of his desk.

I wondered what was going through his mind. Fear? Panic? Remorse? I figured the last one was too much to hope for.

The period seemed to last for hours. I hadn't been able to concentrate on any of my classes. I wondered if I'd be able to pass my courses and be a second-semester junior when I finally got back home.

Home. It seemed a million miles away. If only this were just a bad dream and I could go back to my old life by clicking my heels together and saying, "There's no place like home, there's no place like home."

If only I'd never come! I'd be a happy, carefree person right now, going through my junior year with my friends. I felt a flicker of resentment toward my parents.

But it wasn't their fault. They were trying to save their marriage. How could they know I'd spend an evening in the hills with people who'd kill someone?

"I feel sorry for Heath," Eve said after class. "He seems so strange—and lonely." She smiled ruefully. "I hadn't even noticed he was gone."

"Me either," I lied.

"I'll see you in the journalism room after school, right?" Eve said.

"Right. I'll be there."

I wished I could go home after school. How could I focus on something as trivial as an article for the newspaper when I had death and guilt on my mind?

I forced myself to walk up to the journalism room after school. One foot in front of the other. I stood in the doorway and looked around the classroom.

A dozen or so students milled around the easels and tables that were littered with papers.

"Julia!" Eve hurried over, smiling. "Colin's so glad you're going to work with us!"

I planted a smile on my face. "Hi, Eve."

"Come meet him. He's over talking to the sports photographers."

I followed her to the back of the room where three people talked in a huddle. They studied photos of the football team in action.

"Crop this one here," a tall guy said, pointing to a picture. "It's a good action photo of Matt. We'll use it in the first issue."

"Colin?" Eve said.

The tall guy turned to us. He looked at Eve, then smiled at me.

"This is Julia Bliss," Eve said. "Julia, this is our editor, Colin Maitland."

"Hi," I said.

"Great to have you with us," Colin said. "We need another reporter."

Colin was a good-looking guy, tall with long features.

Long, dark, and handsome.

"I told Eve that I haven't written for a newspaper before," I said.

"Hey, no problem. Everyone's a neophyte at first. You'll catch on. It's not any harder than writing papers for school, and usually a lot more interesting."

I liked Colin right away; he didn't seem like the other guys I'd met in Franklin Heights. He seemed smart. And *nice*. I guessed he wouldn't consider it fun to torture a guy by setting fire to a cabin he was in.

"I was thinking," Eve said. "Maybe Julia could write a piece about what it's like to come here from a large school in another state. You know, kind of compare us with the school she came from."

"Oh, I don't know—" I said.

How could I compare without sounding critical? I hated this school. Well, maybe not the school itself, just the jerks who take classes here.

"That might be interesting," Colin said. "What do you think, Julia?"

"Um, I think I'd rather write about something else," I said.

Colin smiled. "Would we come out smelling like garbage?"

I felt my cheeks flush. "Well, not exactly."

"Think about it. Maybe if you look hard, you'll find some positive things about this school." He gave my arm a gentle squeeze and moved on to talk with a guy behind me.

Hmmm, maybe there would be some positive things here, at that, I thought.

If only I didn't have murder on my conscience.

The meeting didn't take very long. It was led by Colin and Mr. Bellows, the journalism teacher.

Some of the students were already working on pieces: editorials, essays, and articles about school policies and activities. The sales staff reported that local businesses were already buying ads for the first issue.

It was interesting, and it took my mind off Heath Quinn for a little while.

After the meeting, I trudged home, the heaviness and ache back in my chest.

I missed the news at six because Nikki loudly insisted on watching *M*A*S*H* reruns during supper instead. I guess Uncle Jim and Aunt Helen had decided they'd rather give in than have her run from the table again tonight.

I spent the evening in my room—the family guest room—trying to concentrate on my chemistry homework. My mind drifted away, though, every couple of minutes, and it was an effort to pull myself back to the work in front of me. The problems that should normally have taken an hour took nearly twice that long.

The phone rang at nine-thirty.

"Julia!" Aunt Helen called. "It's your mother."

I jumped up from my desk, ran into Aunt Helen's room and picked up the extension.

"Mom?"

"Hi, honey," she said. She sounded sad.

Alarm bells went off in my head. "You okay?"

Oh, please don't let her tell me they're getting a divorce!

"Yes, I'm fine," she said.

But she didn't sound fine.

"How are you doing?" she asked. "Do you need anything?"

Yes, I need you! I need a friend! I need to get out of this horrible town where people are murdered!

"I'm fine," I said.

How could I make her more miserable than she already was?

"How're things with you and Dad?" I asked.

She sighed deeply. "Oh, we just have a lot of things to work out. Are you and Nikki getting along?"

"Pretty well."

"Is there a problem?"

"No. Not really."

"I'm so sorry to do this to you, honey," she said. "I'm sorry you had to leave your friends here."

"Well, it's only for a semester." I said it to remind her of her promise.

"Yes, that's right. Sure you don't need anything?"

"No, I'm fine. But I'm looking forward to coming home."

She would never know how much.

"I think once you get to know the other people there, you'll settle in and be very happy. Nikki was always a nice little girl."

But people change, Mom.

"I like my friends at home better."

"Honey, I have to leave now. Your dad just came in and needs to make a call. I just wanted to let you know we're thinking of you."

"Thanks for calling."

"Bye, honey. Love you."

"Me, too. Bye."

She hung up.

I put the receiver back in place and sat on the bed, staring at the white chenille spread.

Hearing Mom's voice had made me more homesick than ever, homesick for my normal life. It had been a terrible mistake to come here. But even if I could leave now, it wouldn't erase what had happened.

How could I go back and cheer at football games and spend time with my friends, knowing what happened in the hills near Franklin Heights?

How could I ever be normal again?

I got up and trudged back into my room.

Once again, I tried to study, but the words blurred on the page. After more than twenty minutes, I gave up.

The phone rang, and for lack of anything better to do, I hurried to answer it, yelling, "I'll get it!"

I ran back to my aunt and uncle's bedroom and picked up the phone.

"Hello?"

"Julia?" The voice was anxious.

"Yes?"

"This is Eve," she said in a rush. "Turn on your TV! Channel 8. *Right now!*"

I hung up and ran downstairs. I met Nikki on

the stairs. She was watching the news through the stair rails again, but this time when she saw me, she didn't leave. She looked frightened and covered her mouth with one hand.

Aunt Helen and Uncle Jim sat on the couch watching, too.

"You girls know this boy?" Uncle Jim said without looking up.

"Who?" I asked. Of course, I knew who it must be.

"Heath Quinn," Uncle Jim said. "That his name?"

"I think so," said Aunt Helen.

"Seems he's missing," Uncle Jim said. "They're wondering if he's the person who died in that cabin fire in the hills."

4

"Did you see the report about Heath Quinn?"

Eve had called back a few minutes later. I was back in my aunt's room, talking on the phone.

"Yes," I said.

"Don't you think it's strange that Heath's parents waited this long to report him missing?" Eve said.

"Maybe it's not unusual for Heath to disappear for a couple of days," I said.

"Maybe," Eve said. "I heard once his father's an alcoholic and his mother isn't there half the time. I think she supports the family working at the mall."

"Maybe neither of his parents are very tuned in," I said.

"I want to do an article about Heath," Eve said.

I was immediately alert. "We don't know yet that Heath was the person who died in the fire."

"I know," Eve said. "But I think the people at school need to think about how the outsiders feel. I want to write about the kids who are left out. You know, the students who aren't sports heroes and who don't have many friends. The kind of people who get made fun of. I won't have to mention Heath's name. They'll know who I mean."

I remembered how the students in my lit class had laughed at Heath when he'd talked about revenge in "The Cask of Amontillado."

"Yes, they probably *will* know who you mean."

"I feel so sorry for Heath," Eve said. "I hope he wasn't the person killed in the fire, but I guess in a sense, he's dead anyway."

"What do you mean?"

"He's dead to the people at school, and I'm including myself. I hadn't even noticed he'd been gone until Ms. Cater asked about him in class today." She paused. "Anyway, would you like to do the story with me? We could work on it together."

"Yes, I'd like to," I said.

I knew I could concentrate on *this* article.

"Good. Let's talk to Colin tomorrow. I'll meet you in the journalism room before school. I think he'll like the idea."

We said good-bye, and I hung up.

"I heard what you said!"

Nikki stood in the doorway, her face frightened and furious. She stepped into the room and swung the door closed. *"You were talking about Heath!"*

I held up my hands. "That was Eve Lenhart," I said. "She wants to write an article for the school paper."

"Why did she call *you*?"

"She invited me to join *The Bugle* staff, and I said I'd write some articles for them."

"She's going to write about *Heath* in the school paper?" Her face was a deep red.

"Nikki, relax. We're both going to work on an article about Heath. But not about his death. In fact, we aren't even going to mention his name. We're going to write an article about the outsiders. The people who fall between the cracks, who aren't involved in activities and don't have many friends."

Nikki calmed down as I talked.

"You're not mentioning him by name?"

"No."

Nikki expelled a large breath of air. "Okay." She leaned against the door. "They're putting it together. The body and Heath."

"You knew they would."

She started crying then, huge, quiet sobs. "I'm so scared! I don't want to go to jail."

"Neither do I. But Nikki, we have to tell what we know. Think of Heath's parents. Wouldn't you want to know if your son—"

Nikki ran toward me and shoved me hard. "No—*No!* That's easy for you to say. Easy for *you* to feel sorry for his parents! You didn't set fire to the cabin."

"Neither did you," I said. "It was Matt."

"So you're going to throw my boyfriend to the *wolves!*" she cried. "You don't care about my friends any more than you care about me!"

"This has nothing to do about *caring* for your friends!" I said. "Heath Quinn is *dead!*"

She screamed in rage and despair, threw the door open and ran straight into Aunt Helen.

"What's—what's going *on* in here?" she demanded.

"I hate Julia! I *hate* her!" Nikki shrieked. She ran past her mother, disappeared down the hall and into her room.

The door slammed shut.

Aunt Helen looked back at me, horrified.

"What's happened between you two?" she said. "Why is Nikki acting this way?"

"I'm sorry, Aunt Helen," I said. "Nikki just—just had a bad day."

It was one of the most ridiculous things I'd ever said, and I blurted it out without thinking. But what else could I say? I certainly couldn't say, "Nikki's upset because she thinks she's going to be charged with murder."

I forced a smile. Aunt Helen looked at me, bewildered, as I walked past her and back to my room.

"So what do you think?" Eve said.

Eve had just described the article she wanted us to write for *The Bugle*. Colin had listened attentively, nodding as she talked.

"I like it," Colin said. "I think you're on to something very good here." He smiled at us both. "You two are the right reporters to do the story."

"Oh?" Eve said, smiling.

"You have the sensitivity for it. This'll be a good piece."

Eve grinned at me, then back at him. "Thanks," she said. "And we agree."

Colin frowned. "People like Heath have been

shoved around and ignored in this school for too long. Did you see the news last night?''

"That's what gave me the idea," Eve said.

"If the body *is* Heath's," Colin said, "it'll be a short end to a very sad life."

"Did you know him?" Eve asked, surprised. "I mean, *do* you know him?"

"Not as well as I should. That's why this piece should be written for *The Bugle*. Maybe it'll wake people up, and they'll extend themselves a little more to the others who're ignored."

Colin smiled at me again, and I smiled back. I had a feeling that writing for *The Bugle* and my friendship with Eve and Colin were going to help keep me sane this semester.

I sure needed that.

Before we left, Eve and I agreed to meet the next night, Friday, at 7:30 at her house to talk about our article.

I went through the rest of my classes, still not able to focus on discussions or lectures. In lit class, I looked over at Matt. Our eyes met, and he immediately looked away.

That was how the others who had been in the hills that night acted toward me. As if I weren't there.

They were trying to blot it out, pretending it never happened. But they were changed. Instead of making smart remarks in class, Matt stared at his desktop and never opened his mouth.

The others weren't in my classes, but I saw them occasionally in the hall.

That afternoon I saw Sean coming toward me

just outside the gym. He stared straight ahead of him, not looking at anybody.

Mr. Dyer, the football coach, stuck his head out of his office door.

"Wallace!" he barked.

Sean stopped and turned around.

"We've got some talking to do, you and I," the coach said, striding over to Sean. "You'd better work harder in class and on the football field, or you're likely to find your butt off the team and flunking P.E."

I kept walking. Other students had slowed and turned their heads to hear everything they could.

It had to be humiliating for Sean. As far as I knew, football was Sean's only talent. It's what made him a big man around school.

Because of the night in the hills, he wasn't even able to focus on his favorite sport.

On my way to lunch at noon, I spotted Nikki and Matt standing together just inside the cafeteria. Nikki frowned and waved me over.

"Hi," I said. I was surprised she had wanted to see me.

"Tell Matt that you're not going to write about Heath," Nikki said.

Matt looked angry. "What's this crap about you writing an article for *The Bugle*?"

"It won't be about his death," I said. I explained to Matt that the article would focus on the lonely people in school. "I won't even mention his name."

"This whole thing's going to break wide open!" Matt said angrily.

"Shhh!" Nikki said, looking back over her shoulder. "Keep your voice down, Matt! Anyone coming into the cafeteria or standing just outside will hear you."

"You should see Sean on the football field," he said, lowering his voice only a little. "He can't concentrate, and the coach is suspicious. Randy isn't doing much better."

"Brandi's nervous as a cat," Nikki said.

I could have pointed out to Nikki that she was, too, but I didn't.

"We've got to stick together," he went on. "Any one of us could blow it for the others. If your article even comes close to saying anything about the five of us, or if you write about Heath's death"—he pointed a finger in my face—"I'll kill you, you hear? I swear I'll kill you."

A dark figure walked into my peripheral vision and stopped. I turned and saw a dark-haired, attractive guy, probably in his early twenties, staring at us.

"Who's that?" Nikki whispered.

"He doesn't go to school here," Matt said.

"He's too old to be a senior," Nikki said.

The guy turned slowly and walked out of the cafeteria.

"You don't think he heard us, do you?" Nikki said, her hand in front of her mouth.

"I don't know," Matt said, glaring in the direction the guy went. "I don't like the way he looked at us. Keep an eye out for him."

"We should never talk in public about what happened," Nikki whispered. "From now on, we'll only talk about it away from school when no one's around."

"Yeah, that's right," Matt said. "And I'm warning you, Julia. You'd better not write anything that could point to any of us. If you do, you'll never live to write another word."

"Hi, Aunt Helen."

I'd just gotten home from school and found her sitting on the living room couch, reading the morning newspaper.

"Hi, Julia," she said, looking up with a smile. "Hungry?"

"Not very," I said. "I can wait till supper."

"Oh, an envelope was in the mailbox for you today. It didn't have a stamp or postmark, so someone must have left it there."

"Okay."

"Maybe a party invitation," she said.

"Maybe."

"I put it on your bed."

"Thanks."

I took the stairs two at the time and went into my room. The white business envelope sat in the middle of my bed, not looking at all festive the way a party invitation usually looks.

I grabbed the letter opener from my desk and opened the envelope.

Inside was a folded sheet of lined notebook paper. I opened it and stared at what was written on the page.

In capital letters, written by an old typewriter, it said:

YOU TRIED TO KILL ME.
FOR THAT YOU WILL DIE.

The message was horrifying enough. But it was the signature that stopped me cold. It was signed *Heath*.

5

How could this note be from Heath? I thought he was dead!

He *had* died in that fire, hadn't he? If not, how had he survived? Had he escaped through the back window?

And if it wasn't Heath's body that was found in the remains of the cabin, whose was it?

I felt both relief and horror rush through me, along with a powerful surge of adrenalin.

I read the words again. The writer knew I'd been in the hills that night. But he'd said that I'd tried to kill him. Of course, I *hadn't* tried to kill him; in fact, I'd tried to save him.

But maybe Heath was angry because I *hadn't* saved him. Maybe just being with the crowd who had tried to kill him was enough.

And for that, he said I would die.

I walked out of my room on shaky legs and stopped at the top of the stairs.

"Aunt Helen?" I was surprised that I kept my voice from trembling.

"Yes, dear?" Her voice came from the living room.

"Did Nikki get an envelope in the mailbox, too?"

"No, just you. Was it a party invitation?"

"Uh, not exactly. Just a note." I rushed on, so she wouldn't ask more. "What's for supper?"

"Chicken cooked on the grill. Is that okay?"

"Sounds great."

I went back to my room, closed the door and sat on my bed. Nikki hadn't gotten a note. I wondered why.

Could *she* have sent it? Or Matt? Were they so worried I'd expose them in my article, that they'd tried to convince me that Heath hadn't died?

Or were they warning me that they were coming after me?

I put the note in my bedside table drawer under a tissue box.

Then I thought of something and pulled it out again. I looked carefully at the printing. It had been typed on what must have been a very old manual typewriter.

The left half of the *T*s' tops were gone. And the *E*s were so faint, they were nearly invisible.

Had Heath typed this?

I thought I might have a chance to find out. Ms. Cater kept our assigned papers inside folders in a red plastic milk crate behind her desk. So far, we had only turned in one paper.

Heath's should be there if he had done the assignment. If he'd typed the paper on the same typewriter that wrote the threatening note, I should be able to tell by looking at the capital *T*s and *E*s.

I'd have to check when Ms. Cater wasn't there.

I debated about whether to tell Nikki about the note. I figured I could probably guess by watching her face whether she had sent it or known about it. But, at least for now, I decided not to say anything. If Nikki *didn't* know about it, I was sure she'd get hysterical if I told her, and I wasn't in the mood to deal with that tonight.

I decided to wait and check the typing in Heath's writing folder first. After that, I'd decide on my next move.

Madeline Jenkins announced the lead story on the six o'clock news while we ate our grilled chicken dinner in the kitchen.

"An autopsy was performed this morning on the body found at the site of last week's Mann County fire," she said. "County coroner Dr. Max Simpson spoke to reporters this afternoon about his findings. For that report, we'll go to Mandy Richards, who's been covering this story. Mandy?"

Mandy then appeared with her microphone, standing outside the Mann County Hospital.

"Madeline, Dr. Simpson announced this afternoon that the body found last weekend was so badly burned, little remains but bones and teeth. This will make a positive identification more difficult. However, Dr. Simpson was able to determine that the body was that of a young male, probably in his teens or early twenties."

Heath.

I glanced over at Nikki who watched the TV, her hand holding the side of her head.

"Mandy," Madeline said, "has there been further investigation of Heath Quinn, the missing Franklin Heights boy? The sex and age match. Could he have been the person killed in the Mann County fire?"

"That certainly has been in the minds of investigators, Madeline," said Mandy. "So far, they can't say because dental records don't seem to be available on Heath Quinn. The boy's parents can't remember ever taking their son to a dentist."

"That's interesting." Madeline sounded surprised.

"It certainly leaves investigators with a puzzle on their hands," Mandy said.

Aunt Helen sighed. "Oh, I hope it wasn't that young boy from your school. How tragic."

"Sure is," Uncle Jim said. "He's too young to die."

The news team went on to report other stories. Aunt Helen and Uncle Jim continued eating and watching TV. Nikki and I picked at our food. Nikki stared at her plate, but never once glanced up during the meal.

"Thanks, Aunt Helen, that was good," I said when we were finished.

"You didn't eat much," she said. "Neither did you, Nikki."

Nikki rolled her eyes and left the table without saying anything. I went up to my room and tried to concentrate on homework.

Nikki drove us to school the next day. We usually rode together in the morning in an effort to look as if we were getting along. But I always found a reason not to come home when she did so I could avoid her.

That's the way she wanted it, too. It was a game we played every day.

"I have a meeting after school at *The Bugle*," I said. "I'll see you at home later."

She didn't answer, but got out of the car and slammed the door shut. We walked in silence up the sidewalk to the school, through the front door and up the stairs to the second floor.

Our lockers were in the same hallway about twenty feet apart. She went to her locker, and I went to mine. The corridor was busy with people walking to their classes, opening locker doors and slamming them.

I put the books from last night's homework on the shelf and pulled out what I'd need for this morning's classes. I closed the door.

That's when I heard the shriek. Nikki ran over to me, her face wild with panic.

"Come here!" she squealed at me. She grabbed my sleeve and pulled.

"I'm coming! Let go!"

People were staring.

I yanked my arm out of her grasp and followed her down the hall and into the ladies' room. Only one stall was occupied.

She thrust a white envelope into my hand.

"Look at *this!*" she whispered.

I knew immediately what it was. Another threatening note written on notebook paper by the same old typewriter.

It had the identical message.

"I got one, too," I said. "Delivered to the mailbox at your house."

"When?"

"Yesterday afternoon."

Her eyes got big, and she whispered fiercely in my face, *"And you didn't tell me?"* She grabbed the paper away and shook it at me.

"This means—" She looked back over her shoulder at the occupied stall and softened her voice till it was inaudible. She mouthed the words: "This means Heath is *alive!*"

"I know," I whispered back. "*If* it's from Heath."

"No one else knows what happened!" she whispered. She stared at me. "Unless you told."

"I didn't—"

The stall door opened and a girl I didn't recognize came out. She hooked her bookbag over her shoulder, barely glanced at us, washed her hands and left.

"You didn't tell anyone?" Nikki said.

"No one."

"Then this *has* to be from Heath!" She turned and paced around the ladies' room, staring at the paper. "And he says he's going to kill me! What can I *do?* I can't call the police!" She stopped and looked at me. "Do you think he means this? Is he going to try and kill me?"

"There's no way to tell."

"Well, you're a lot of help!"

"Nikki, you're asking me to make predictions based on . . . on nothing but a piece of paper! We don't even know that Heath typed this note!"

"I wonder if the others got notes," she said.

"I'm sure we'll hear about it if they did."

"Why did he deliver yours to the house and mine to my locker?"

"I don't know. Was the note taped to the locker door?"

"No," she said. "It was folded up on the floor. He must have pushed the note in through the slits in the door."

"I think for now, we shouldn't mention the notes to the others."

"I'm going to tell Matt."

"Wait and see if Matt gets a note."

"What are you thinking?" she said. "That *Matt* typed the notes?"

"I just want to see what happens—"

The door opened and a math teacher walked in.

"I'm going to tell him," Nikki said angrily. "And I'm going to tell him you think *he* wrote the notes!"

She turned and stalked out.

Everyone at school was talking about Heath as if he were dead. They'd heard the news report last night and assumed he was the person who'd been killed in the fire. They all had comments about him. Mostly, though, they just thought he was weird.

After school, I waited about twenty minutes, then went to Ms. Cater's room, hoping she wasn't in. I peeked into the classroom.

Ms. Cater was sitting at her desk, hunched over a pile of papers. She looked up.

"Hi, Julia."

"Hi," I said. I almost ducked back out the door, but something kept me from doing it.

"You looking for me?"

I made a quick decision.

"Well, Eve Lenhart and I are going to write an article for *The Bugle* about... well... about the kids at school that don't fit in."

She smiled thoughtfully and nodded.

"I mean, the ones who aren't particularly good students or good athletes."

"We do have people like that here," she said.

"Some of them seem very lonely," I said.

Ms. Cater nodded again. "We have one in your class."

"Heath Quinn."

"Did you see the news last night?" she asked.

"Yes," I said.

"Are you going to write about Heath?"

"Not specifically."

"Even if the body turns out to be his?"

"We hadn't planned on it," I said.

"I think you should."

"Why?"

She scooted her chair back from her desk. "Come here. Let me show you something," she said.

I walked to her desk.

She reached around to the plastic milk box behind her with the file folders full of student writing.

Was she going to show me Heath's paper?

She fingered the tabs at the tops of the folders and pulled one out.

"This is Heath's first paper for this class," she said. "I think you should read it."

I looked at the paper and the typing on the page.

It had been written on an old manual typewriter. The left top of the capital Ts were gone and the capital Es were almost not visible.

It took a second to hit me: *Heath was alive!*

~6

I sat on my bed holding Heath's paper from lit class. The title was "Mr. Bigelow: A Study in Loneliness."

Our class had read a dozen short stories and had been asked to write an essay about one of them. Heath had chosen Ray Bradbury's story, "The Dwarf." It's about a little guy, a dwarf named Mr. Bigelow, who comes every day to the carnival and pays his money so he can go into the tent with the warped mirrors that show him to be very tall.

Mr. Bigelow is harassed and made fun of by Ralph Banghart, the guy who runs the tent with the mirror maze.

Mr. Bigelow knows what it is to be left out, Heath wrote. *He knows the tragedy of loneliness, of being different, of not fitting in. He knows what it's like to be humiliated by someone who is less of a human being than he is, someone like Ralph Banghart, who is the true dwarf in the story because of his small, twisted heart.*

I read the whole paper once, then I read it over again. Heath had identified with the dwarf in the story, who was either a person to ridicule or an object of pity to the other characters.

But what Mr. Bigelow didn't understand, Heath wrote, *is that the answer to cruelty isn't self-punishment. He hid himself away from everyone, taking the humiliation and ridicule that everyone heaped on him—until he couldn't take it anymore. He chose suicide to punish himself for the injustices he suffered, as if they were his fault. Instead, he should have struck out at his tormenters and killed them all for their hatred and cruelty.*

I thought about Heath and what he'd said in class that day about revenge, that "hate and revenge are the most powerful forces in the universe."

Heath was still alive and threatening to kill the people who'd been in the hills that night.

I had no doubt that he'd do it.

At least, he would try.

I got up, laid his paper on my desk, and sat in my chair.

I'd been so surprised to find out that Heath was alive, I hadn't had much time to think about the next logical question: *If Heath was alive, whose body had been found in the cabin?*

Could it have been the hobo we'd seen earlier? He'd run off ahead of us into the trees. He could easily have gotten there before we did. Maybe he'd been using the cabin as a home.

Really, the body could have been anybody's.

Maybe it was someone who had already been dead. It would certainly make me feel better to know that the fire hadn't killed the guy.

But I was rationalizing.

I heard running steps in the hallway. Nikki burst into my room and slammed the door behind her.

"Matt got a note today, too!" she said, breathlessly. "Everyone did! Heath's alive, and now he's going to *kill* us!"

I couldn't argue with her this time.

"I think we should get everyone together," I said. "Tell them we'll meet tonight."

"Where?"

"How about the baseball diamond at the park?"

"What time?"

I had to see Eve at 7:30. The meeting would have to be earlier. "After supper about six-thirty."

"I'll get hold of everyone," she said and ran into her mother's room to make the first call.

All of us had gotten threatening notes. If Heath was as serious about revenge as he'd said he was, he would certainly come after us. Even me. And why not? I'd failed to help him at the cabin, and I hadn't gone to the police afterward.

I was as guilty as the others.

Nikki and I drove to the baseball diamond at 6:30 P.M. Matt and Randy were already there, sitting on the bleachers. Brandi arrived a few minutes later.

"Where's Sean?" Nikki said.

Matt shrugged.

He didn't look good. His face had a day's worth of whiskers, and there were bags under his eyes. He kept his arms folded and stared at the ground.

"So what are we going to do about Heath?" Nikki looked at me.

"I think we should wait for Sean," I said. "He should be here soon."

"He's always late," Nikki complained. "We should decide what to do and tell him after he gets here."

"What do you think?" I asked, looking around at the others.

Brandi and Randy nodded.

Matt shrugged. "I don't care," he said. "Let's get this over with."

"You all got notes?" I asked. "Where were they delivered?"

"Mine was in my mailbox at home," Brandi said.

"Gym locker," said Randy.

I looked at Matt.

He sighed loudly. "What difference does it make? We all got notes."

"I don't *know* what difference it makes now," I said. "Maybe it doesn't matter. But I think we should collect information. Maybe we'll need it later. Where did you find your note?"

"My gym locker." He didn't look at me.

"When would be the easiest time to get into the guys' locker room without being seen?" I asked.

Randy scratched his ear. "During football practice," he said. "The room is open but usually nobody's there."

"Did either of you see anyone resembling Heath near the building yesterday during practice?" I asked them.

Matt scowled. "Are you kidding? We're busy during practice. We're over on the field. We can't even *see* the locker room door from there."

"Do you remember anyone leaving practice early?" I asked.

"Oh, cut the *Murder, She Wrote* crap," Nikki said, scowling. "I want to know what we're going to do to *protect* ourselves. My dad has a hunting rifle—"

"We don't need guns," I said.

"Since when are you making the decisions around here, Julia?" Nikki said. "If I want to have a gun with me, I'll do it, and I don't give a rat's butt what you think."

"How do we know for sure that Heath wrote those notes?" Randy asked.

"Of course, Heath wrote them," Nikki said. "Who else knows what happened?"

"I'm pretty sure Heath wrote them," I said.

"Mrs. Fletcher strikes again," Nikki muttered.

I ignored her. "I checked the typewritten letters in my note with a paper he wrote for lit class. They were written on the same typewriter."

"Who cares about the typewriter!" Nikki said. "We've got to get rid of him before he kills us."

"Then you *would* deserve prison," I said. "What we need to do is find Heath and talk to him."

"Talk to him!" Nikki shrieked. "He's just threatened to *kill* each one of us, and you want to *talk* to him?"

"Maybe Julia's right," Matt said.

"What?"

"Shut up, Nikki," he said. "Maybe we should

53

find him and explain that we were all drunk that night, that we didn't mean it."

Nikki glared at Matt and he stared back at her.

"Maybe," Brandi said.

"So how do we find him?" Randy asked.

"Let me work on it, okay?" I said. "I'm writing an article for *The Bugle*—"

"We already know that, Julia," Nikki snapped.

"I can find out about him without attracting attention if I'm working on the article."

"But whatever you find out," Matt said, "you have to bring back to the group."

I shrugged. "That's fair. And if any of you hear anything, bring it back here."

"Okay," they said.

"Meanwhile," Matt said, "we've got to keep cool. Sean's about to lose it, and the coach is getting suspicious."

"Do you think he'll *tell?*" Nikki looked panicked.

"He'd better not," Matt said.

"Where *is* he, anyway?" Nikki said.

"You called him, right?" Brandi said.

"Yeah. I called everybody."

"And he said he'd come?" Randy asked.

Nikki nodded. "He said he'd meet us at six-thirty. He seemed so spooked, I thought he'd be the first one here."

Matt took Nikki's arm. "Let's get out of here. I've had enough."

"Okay," she said.

We all got up from the bleacher seats.

"Wait," Brandi said, taking hold of Nikki's other arm.

"What?"

"Take a look across the field, near the swings."

We all turned and looked.

"There's a guy in a brown jacket taking pictures," Brandi said. "He's taking pictures of *us!*"

Nikki gasped. "He's got a big lens on his camera!"

"It's that guy who was in the school cafeteria the other day," Matt said. "He must've heard what we said! He's *following* us!"

"Turn your backs," Randy said.

We turned so he couldn't photograph our faces. I felt like a criminal; I was sure *acting* guilty.

"I'm going to kill that guy!" Matt said. "Randy, let's rush him. We'll teach him not to butt into other people's lives!"

"He might have a gun or something," Nikki said. "Leave him alone."

Matt ignored her. "Come on, Randy. Are you ready?"

"No!" Nikki cried.

"Well, I guess," Randy said.

"Now!" Matt said.

They both turned around and tore off in the direction of the swings.

"Where is he?" Nikki said.

The man had vanished.

Matt and Randy slowed their pace, then stopped. "Where did he go?" Matt said.

"What a coward," Randy said.

They walked back to Brandi, Nikki, and me.

"Let's get out of here," Nikki said.

"I'll walk," I said. "I'm going to Eve's."

Without another word, the four of them left.

I had more than a half hour to kill before meeting Eve at her house, so I sat on the bleachers at the baseball diamond. The guy with the camera was not in sight.

Who *was* he?

Probably no one, I thought. We're feeling guilty, so we assume he came after us. He was probably taking pictures of the oak trees on the hill behind us. Maybe he happened to be in the cafeteria the other day looking for a brother or sister who was a student there.

I breathed in deeply the fresh autumn air and wished I were at home with my friends.

My friends who didn't murder people, who didn't even get into much trouble.

True friends I could count on.

Once again, I ached for home and my old life. It had seemed so ordinary and unexciting at one time. If only I had it back again.

My thoughts turned to Nikki and the others.

I didn't trust Matt. I didn't believe that he wanted to find Heath and just talk. I think he wanted me to find Heath for him so he could—well, I didn't know for sure what he wanted to do. But I was afraid he wanted to kill Heath, just as Nikki did.

I had no intention of telling Matt or Nikki or anyone else what I might learn about Heath's whereabouts.

A movement, a flash of brown at the edge of my vision, interrupted my thoughts. It disappeared behind a small white building next to the playing field.

Someone was there.

I was curious. I got up and started walking toward the building.

I hadn't seen the mysterious man with the camera come back, and it didn't occur to me that I might be in danger.

The structure was probably used as a concession stand during baseball games in the summer, I thought. It was small, taking up only about twelve square feet. But it was big enough for somebody to hide behind.

All at once I thought of Heath. Could this be Heath behind the building? Had he followed me or one of the others to the park and watched us?

Or had the guy with the camera taken off his brown jacket and stayed around to watch me?

I remembered Heath's jacket, the beige one he'd been wearing that night in the hills. Was the flash of beige I'd just seen the same as that jacket?

I couldn't be sure, but it was similar.

I kept walking toward the building. I realized vaguely that my hands were wet. I wiped them on my jeans.

"Heath?" I said. I spoke the name quietly, but clearly enough so that someone behind the building could hear it.

No answer.

"Is that you, Heath?"

Again, there was no answer.

I stepped carefully around to the side of the building. No one was there.

"Heath? I'd like to talk to you."

Had I imagined seeing something? It had only been in my peripheral vision. Maybe I was so nervous about the threatening notes that I'd assumed something was there. Maybe a branch had waved in the breeze. Maybe it was something that simple.

"Heath?"

I came around the corner to the front of the building.

The door was open a few inches. Someone was inside. Maybe just a park maintenance worker.

Of course. That had to be who was there.

"Hello?"

I took a few more steps. A sound to the side of the door startled me.

The cashier's window slid open an inch.

The barrel of a gun poked out.

An animal noise came out of my mouth. Did I make that sound? I don't remember much about the next moment, except that I ran.

I ducked behind the concession stand and tore across the baseball field, faster than I'd ever run in my life.

7

I waited for the blast of the gun, but I heard nothing. Nothing except the sound of my own footsteps running through the grass in the park. I ran over the ground past the playground, past the empty swimming pool, the picnic benches, and on through a stand of oak trees.

I didn't stop until I reached the edge of the park. I looked back over my shoulder.

No one was chasing me.

Who was inside the concession stand with a gun? If it was Heath, why didn't he fire at me?

Maybe it wasn't Heath. Maybe it was a kid with a toy gun trying to scare me.

He'd done a good job.

My heart was still hammering hard when I walked down the street where Eve lived. I slowed my pace and took a couple of deep breaths. Then I walked a couple of blocks out of the way and back again. I didn't want to look like a scared animal when I got there.

It took another five minutes to reach her house, an older two-story home with a big front porch. I climbed the porch steps and rang the bell.

In less than a half-minute, the door was pulled open. Eve pushed open the screen door.

"Hi, Julia. Come on in." She smiled and led me into the living room.

Colin got up from a large, squatting chair. "Hi, Julia."

My pulse quickened. Just when I had finally gotten it down to an almost normal rate. But I forgave him.

"Oh, hi, Colin," I said as casually as I could manage. "I didn't know you were going to be here."

"He just arrived," Eve said.

"Do you mind?" Colin asked.

"No," I said, grinning like an idiot. "I'm just surprised. Not many people want to work on a Friday night."

"Colin and I were talking about the article today at school," Eve said. "So I asked him if he wanted to come over and finish the conversation with both of us. You guys want sodas?"

"Diet Coke?" I asked. Eve nodded.

"Regular Coke," Colin said. He turned to me. "Eve has some good ideas."

"Sit down, Julia," Eve said. "Colin, tell her what we've been talking about." She disappeared toward the back of the house.

I sat on the couch. Colin went back to his chair.

"In light of what the coroner came up with," Colin said, "Eve thought you should focus the article on Heath Quinn—I mean, *naming* him—and I agree."

I stared back at Colin.

"Did I miss something?" I said. "The report said the body was that of a young male, but no one could identify it as being Heath's."

"Yes, that's true. A lack of dental records. Heath didn't have any."

"Didn't that seem strange to you?" I said. "I mean, don't most people go to the dentist *sometime* in the first seventeen years of their life?"

"I suppose," Colin said.

"I've heard his dad's an alcoholic," I said.

"The rumor mill in this town is alive and well," Colin said grimly.

"It isn't true?" I asked.

"I don't know," Colin said. "I just get tired of the people in this town passing along unsubstantiated rumors."

"You and Eve think we should write an article about Heath's death?"

I remembered Matt's threat about what would happen if I wrote about Heath. He'd kill me.

I'd been hearing that a lot lately.

"You wouldn't have to draw any conclusions," Colin said. "Eve wants to write about Heath's loneliness and how people treated him. His disappearance would be part of the article."

I considered that. I didn't believe that Matt would kill me if I mentioned Heath in the article. He'd been scared and blowing off steam when he'd threatened me. Besides, maybe I could make him see that it would be a good way to ask around about Heath without making anyone suspicious about my curiosity. Maybe I could learn something that might help find him.

"Okay," I said. "That sounds all right to me." I'd have to figure out later how to tell Nikki and Matt.

Colin glanced back over his shoulder toward the kitchen, then back at me.

"Julia, there's a good movie called *Proven Guilty* playing at the mall theater. Would you like to go tomorrow night?"

"Sounds great," I said.

That was when I realized he hadn't smiled since I'd walked in. I smiled, trying to get a sympathetic smile back.

"Good," he said seriously. "I'll pick you up tomorrow at eight-thirty."

Eve came in carrying three soda cans and a bowl of Chex Mix on a tray.

"So, Julia, what do you think about the article idea?"

"Focusing on Heath? I think it's good." I took the Diet Coke she handed me. "But—what if we find out that it wasn't Heath who died in the cabin? What if Heath is still alive?"

"Still alive?" Eve said. "Do you know something I don't?"

"What if it's just a coincidence that Heath disappeared and the body of a guy Heath's age was discovered?" I said. "What if Heath just took off somewhere?"

"And some other guy died in the fire?" she said.

"Right. I heard there are a lot of hobos up in the hills."

"Well, that wouldn't have anything to do with the article, since we're not going to draw conclusions about whether Heath is still alive."

"You think the article might embarrass Heath when he gets back?" I said. "I mean, *if* he gets back? We'd be writing about how lonely he is."

"I see what you mean," Eve said. She turned to Colin. "What do you think?"

"I think we should go ahead with the article," he said. "You can write it so that he doesn't look like a pathetic person. Talk to his teachers. You might be surprised at what you learn. He was in one of my classes last year. He was quiet, but I had a feeling he was a very bright guy."

"I've already talked to Ms. Cater," I said. "She gave me a paper he wrote about loneliness."

"Great!" Eve said. "Maybe we can use part of it!"

"He did a good job," I said.

Colin got up. "Good. I'll let you two work. See you later." He gave me a tiny smile and left.

A tiny smile was better than nothing.

"I think Colin likes you," Eve said.

"You don't mind, do you?" I asked.

"Me? No. I gave up on him last year."

I grinned. "Good, because he asked me to a movie tomorrow."

Eve's face darkened for a moment, then she smiled a little. "Well, that didn't take long. And at my house, too."

Eve *did* mind. That was obvious. But what could I do about it? It wasn't as if I was taking him away from her.

But I didn't want to lose the only friend I'd made in Franklin Heights.

"I'm sorry, Eve," I said. "I didn't know—"

"About my crush?" She shrugged. "That's okay. I'll get over it. I only dream about him every night." She looked at me and laughed. "Just kidding!"

She wasn't kidding.

"Come on," she said, "let's outline the article. I'm sure it'll change as we find out more about Heath. But let's decide on an approach for now."

"Good," I said.

We settled down to work.

The house seemed awfully quiet when I got back home at 10:30. I found Nikki in her room listening to CDs. She didn't even look up when I came in.

"Where are Aunt Helen and Uncle—"

"Out."

I shrugged and went to my bedroom. I pulled my oversized T-shirt out of the drawer and went into the bathroom to take a shower.

I'd just taken off my shirt when the doorbell rang.

"Can you get that, Nikki?" I called out. "I'm going to take a shower."

I heard Nikki stomp out of her room and down the stairs. The door opened below.

"Matt, what's wrong?"

I couldn't hear what he said, but he sounded upset and frightened.

"Julia!" Nikki screamed. *"Get down here!"*

I pulled my shirt back on and raced downstairs.

Nikki turned to me, her face drained of color. *"He's dead!"*

"Who?"

"Sean's dead!" she said. *"Somebody killed him!"*

8

"How do you know Sean's dead?" I asked.

"Tell her," Nikki said to Matt.

"The cops showed up at my house," he said. "Said they were talking to Sean's friends."

"He was shot," Nikki said. "His father found him in the garage."

"When?"

"When he came home from work about six," Matt said.

"*See?*" Nikki said. "Heath said he was going to kill us, and Sean was his first victim!"

"What did the police ask you?" I asked Matt.

Matt sighed heavily. "Were we friends, did he have any enemies that I knew of, did he have a fight with anyone lately, did he owe money to anyone, was he into drugs, what was his home life like—that kind of crap."

"Did you think the cops know anything?" Nikki asked. "I mean, about what happened at the cabin?"

"No," he said.

"Maybe we should send the cops an anonymous

letter telling them that Heath is alive, and he killed Sean," Nikki said.

"That's too dangerous," Matt said. "The cops have ways of tracking down stuff like that. What we have to do is protect ourselves."

"I'm getting out my dad's rifle," Nikki said. She turned to me. "And you'd better keep your mouth shut about it!"

"Call Randy and Brandi," Matt said, "and tell them to get over here. We'd better tell them about Sean."

"The cops could've already talked to Randy," Nikki said. "They were friends. You don't think he'd spill the beans about Heath, do you?"

"They're not asking about Heath," Matt said irritably. "They're asking about Sean. I'm not sure Sean and Heath even knew each other."

"I'll call them right now." Nikki ran into the kitchen, leaving Matt and me standing by the front door.

Matt stood silently and stared at the floor.

"I'm sorry about Sean," I said. "I know he was a good friend of yours."

Matt grunted something unintelligible.

We stood in awkward silence while Nikki's voice drifted in from the kitchen.

"Come over right now," Nikki said urgently. "Something terrible has happened, and we'll tell you when you get here. Bring Randy with you. *Hurry!*"

Nikki returned to the foyer. "Randy was at Brandi's house. They're coming right over. I didn't tell them anything."

Nikki paced back and forth, into the living room and back. She stopped abruptly, then hurried to the front door and locked the deadbolt.

"We need to keep this locked at all times!" she said. "When the doorbell rings, look out the window to make sure it's them."

"Okay," I said.

"Heath's on a killing rampage!" she said, pacing the floor again. "He'll get to us soon! One down and five to go!"

"Will you *sit down?*" Matt said. "You're driving me crazy!"

"I'm driving *you* crazy?" she snapped. "You're the one who got us into this mess in the first place."

"What're you talking about?"

"*You* were the bright guy who started the fire on the cabin porch."

"I don't remember your trying to stop me!" he said ferociously.

"It was *your* stupid idea! You thought it would be so much fun to set fire to the cabin."

"I didn't know the whole thing would go up in flames!" he yelled. "I thought he'd come out running!"

"You're an idiot!"

Matt screamed a filthy word in Nikki's face, then turned around and grabbed the front doorknob.

"It's locked, you moron!" Nikki hollered.

Matt pounded his fist on the door in a rage, twisted the lock, threw the door open, and strode out into the night.

Nikki locked the door again, glared at me and walked into the kitchen.

I waited in the living room until Randy and Brandi rang the bell.

"Look out the window before you open that door!" Nikki yelled from the kitchen. She ran into the room, pushed me aside, peeked out the long window next to the door, and yanked the door open.

She grabbed Brandi's arm and pulled her into the room. Randy followed.

"Did the cops talk to either of you?" she asked.

"The cops?" Brandi said. "What for?

"Sean's dead!" Nikki said. "Somebody shot him!"

"Sean!" Brandi gasped. Her eyes filled with tears. "He's *dead?*"

"And we will be, too, if we don't find Heath first," Nikki said wildly.

"You think Heath killed Sean?" Randy said.

"Who *else* would kill Sean? Heath wrote all of us notes saying we were going to die!" Nikki was getting louder and louder.

Brandi turned to me. "Do you think Heath will come after all of us?"

"I don't know," I said. "But we'd better be very careful."

"He got Sean in his garage," Nikki said. "So stay out of your garage."

"Don't be alone if that's possible," I said. "Try to hang around with someone who's not involved in this. Heath is only interested in revenge. He won't hurt an innocent person."

Nikki's lip curled. "You mean, like *you*, Julia?"

"I don't think Heath considers me an innocent person," I said.

But I wondered: was that why I didn't get shot tonight at the park? Did Heath spare me because I'd tried to stop Matt from setting the fire?

"Yeah, well, I'm going to get my dad's rifle," Nikki said. "I'm not taking any chances."

She disappeared down the hallway, and I heard the basement door open and close.

"I'm getting out my hunting rifle," Randy said. "I've heard Heath's got an old Winchester."

"We don't need guns!" I said.

"If Sean had had a gun," Brandi said, "he might not have gotten killed!"

"Sean wasn't expecting Heath to walk up behind him in the garage," I said. "Even a gun wouldn't have saved him. Being alone is what got him killed."

Footsteps tromped up the stairs, and the basement door opened.

"I've got to get some ammunition," Nikki said, walking into the living room, waving the rifle around in the air. "I can't find where my dad keeps it."

"Point that thing at the floor!" I ordered. "And be careful not to blow your foot off!"

"How can I blow my foot off if I don't have any bullets?" she snapped.

The thought of Nikki with a gun—a loaded gun—was terrifying. She had all the sense and maturity of a seven-year-old.

A sound came from the back of the house.

"What was that?" Nikki said, whirling around, pointing the gun in the direction of the back door.

The back door opened and Uncle Jim stood in the doorway. He saw Nikki and instinctively took a step backwards, throwing his hands back in a protective gesture toward Aunt Helen.

"What the—*Nikki, put that rifle down!*" he hollered.

Nikki rolled her eyes. "It's not loaded."

Uncle Jim rushed to her and grabbed the gun away from her. "Where the hell did you get this?"

"Out of your gun cabinet."

"I thought it was locked," he said and charged down to the basement.

Aunt Helen stood in the middle of the family room, her mouth hanging open in surprise.

"Why in the world did you get out your father's rifle?" she asked.

"I was just showing it to Randy and Brandi," she whined.

"Nikki, you have been told many times since you were a little girl—"

"I'm *not* a little girl anymore!" she shrieked.

"Well, I guess we'll be going," Randy mumbled, stepping sideways toward the door.

"Bye, Nikki," Brandi said.

I let them out, closed and locked the door behind them, then headed upstairs, leaving Nikki and her mother still standing in the middle of the family room floor.

I sat at my desk and stared at a blank piece of paper. I'd told Eve I'd write the introduction to our article about Heath, but I didn't know how to start.

My mind wandered.

Poor Sean. I'd hardly known him. The only time I ever spent with him was that night. I felt sorry for him even though he'd helped start the fire at the cabin.

Sean hadn't exactly been my favorite person, but after all, he hadn't been trying to *kill* Heath up in the hills that night. He'd just been stupid and drunk. He hadn't been thinking clearly.

My mind turned to Heath.

Where was he? Where was he sleeping at night? How was he living?

Could a person live on vengeance? Was that enough to fuel body and soul? Surely, he had to surface occasionally to buy food. Why hadn't anyone in town spotted him? Where did he get the money to buy food? Or did he steal it?

I tapped my pencil on the paper in front of me.

At least Nikki didn't have the gun anymore. That was one less thing I had to worry about. Aunt Helen and Uncle Jim had been horrified that she'd taken it from the gun cabinet. They didn't seem to have a clue about what kind of person Nikki had become. How had they gotten so out of touch with her?

I was very tired all of a sudden. I put the pencil down. Maybe the words would come more easily tomorrow.

I heard Aunt Helen and Uncle Jim go into their bedroom and close the door. I took my big pajama T-shirt into the bathroom, showered, and got ready for bed.

Tomorrow night I'd have my movie date with Colin. That was something pleasant to look forward to.

The house was quiet when I finally turned off the light and slid down under the covers. I didn't want to think about Sean or Heath, so I made myself think of a deep fog that was too thick to see through. I consciously relaxed my muscles and felt myself sinking deeper into the mattress.

A loud scream sent a chill up my spine, and I sat up abruptly in bed, adrenaline coursing through my bloodstream.

"Nikki!" Aunt Helen's voice called out over running footsteps down the hall.

Nikki continued to scream as I leaped out of bed, yanked open my bedroom door, and followed my aunt and uncle through the darkness.

Uncle Jim reached Nikki's bedroom first, pushed the door open, and turned on the light. We rushed in to see Nikki standing in the middle of the room, gaping at the window.

"It was a nightmare. It must have been a nightmare," Aunt Helen said in a soothing voice. She put her arm around Nikki.

Nikki shoved her aside and rushed to the window. "It wasn't a dream! He was right outside my window!"

"Who, Nikki?" Aunt Helen asked. "Who was outside the window?"

"Heath!" she cried. *"I saw him! It was Heath Quinn!* He was here at my window!" She turned to me. "He was here to kill me, I know it!"

9

I didn't get a chance to talk to Nikki because Uncle Jim gave her a sleeping pill and Aunt Helen sat with her until she fell asleep. I went back to bed.

Uncle Jim and Aunt Helen hadn't believed that she'd seen Heath Quinn at her window. They thought all the news reports had upset her and she'd had a nightmare about him.

I was sure Nikki was right, though, that Heath had climbed onto the garage roof to try and get in. Had he planned to murder her in her sleep, then move on through the house to find and kill me?

These thoughts turned over in my mind while I lay awake, staring up into the darkness. I didn't sleep much that night.

As soon as the purple dawn peeked around the edge of the window shade, I got up, dressed quickly, and hurried downstairs. I slipped out the front door and around to the garage.

I found immediately what I was looking for.

A crate from the garage had been dragged around and placed on the overturned garbage can. Heath had built himself a ladder to get to the roof.

I wished I had looked out the window as soon as I'd reached Nikki's room last night. I might have caught a glimpse of him disappearing over the edge of the roof.

I put the crate back in the garage, set the garbage can upright, and headed back into the house.

I fixed myself a bowl of cereal and sat down at the kitchen table.

"Heath was going to kill me last night."

I looked up to see Nikki standing in the kitchen doorway. Her eyes were still blurry from the effects of the sleeping pill.

"I could have been murdered," she said.

"He built himself a ladder to the second floor," I said. I told her about finding the crate on the overturned garbage can.

"Nikki," I said, "did you get a good look at his face?"

"I think he was wearing a stocking over his head. His features were mashed together."

"How do you know for sure it was Heath?"

"It was Heath."

"But you didn't get a good look—"

"I was scared," she said. "I didn't study his face."

"How come your shade wasn't down?"

"I always sleep with the shades up. I pull the shades down while I change. Then when I'm ready for bed, I pull them up and then turn off the light. I like to wake up with the sun shining through the window."

"So you were standing next to the window when you pulled up the shade and saw him?"

"He was staring right at me. And he was wearing that beige jacket he had on the night he was killed. I was so scared."

Mostly to myself, I said, "How did he escape that fire? I can't figure it out."

"And now he's killing us—all of us who were in the hills that night. Sean was the first one to die."

Nikki sat and gazed out the window over my shoulder and spoke softly. "I was supposed to be second." Her face was white and thin; she chewed on her lower lip and blinked, staring into the distance. "If only I could kill him first," she murmured.

"Nikki," I said, "we need to find Heath and try and talk some sense into him."

She didn't respond, but stared with glassy eyes out the window.

I got up and went back to my room. Now I was really tired, so I lay down and fell asleep.

When I woke up it was early afternoon. I tried to begin my article about Heath, but once again, the words eluded me.

What I needed, I thought, was more information about Heath.

That's when I got the idea. *Why hadn't I thought of that before?* Eve and I should talk to Heath's parents! Maybe while they talked about their son, they would tell us something that would help me find him!

I called Eve and told her my idea. She liked it and said she'd try to reach the Quinns to set up an interview.

"I knew I'd picked the right person to do this article with me," she said. "I'll let you know if I reach them."

She didn't call back all afternoon. I had supper with Nikki's family. Nikki insisted again on watching *M*A*S*H* reruns, so we didn't see the news, which certainly would have reported Sean's death.

After supper I changed into a new pair of Levis and a red sweater for my date with Colin.

He rang the doorbell at exactly 8:30.

"I'll get it!"

I hurried down the stairs and opened the door.

Colin looked great. The brown sweater matched his eyes exactly.

He smiled. "How're you doing?"

"Great." Okay, so I'm not a master of comebacks.

"Ready to go?"

"Sure." I called out good-bye to Aunt Helen, and we walked down the sidewalk to the dark blue Volvo parked at the curb.

"Wow. Is this your car?" I asked.

"My dad's," Colin said, smiling. "I borrowed it."

"Nice."

He shrugged. "It'll get us where we're going."

We drove to the movie theater and parked in the middle of the crowded lot.

"Do you want it locked?" I asked, getting out my side.

"I'll lock it from here," he said.

We went in, got our tickets, then chose two seats in the middle of the theater. Even though there were still ten minutes before the show started, it was filling up fast.

"I hear this is a good movie," Colin said. "Roger Ebert gave it a thumbs up."

I shifted uncomfortably in my seat, beginning to feel sorry that I'd had so much iced tea with supper. Now I really had to go to the bathroom.

"Want some popcorn?" Colin asked.

Saved by the popcorn.

"I'd love some," I said. "But I need to use the rest room, so I'll come, too."

We left our jackets on the seats, squeezed past five people in our row, and walked out to the lobby.

I headed for the rest room; he went to the concession counter.

When I came out of the bathroom, Colin was talking to a kid near the front door. He had an arm wrapped around a large tub of popcorn and had balanced one soda cup on top of the other.

"Let me take those," I said. I took the sodas.

The boy smiled, nodded to Colin, then walked over to the concession counter.

"Who's the kid?" I asked.

"Jason Richfield," he said. "Brother of a friend of mine. Smart as a whip."

"Cute, too."

Colin gave me a wry smile. "You think so? His brother thinks he looks a little like me."

I laughed. "You're both cute, but he doesn't look a thing like you."

He laughed. "Come on," he said. "Let's go watch the movie."

Proven Guilty was a good movie. It was about a

guy who had been found guilty of murder. He escaped before the police could take him to prison, and he spent most of the movie trying to prove his innocence. This film had a happy ending, as most of them do, and the hero was freed in the last scene.

I wish life were that simple, I thought, as we walked back to the car after the movie. Of course, in my *real-life* murder story, the main characters are guilty. There are no good guys in my story.

"Feel like a pizza?" Colin asked.

"I'm pretty full from the popcorn," I said.

"Oh, you can manage a slice of pizza," he said, grinning. "Come on. There isn't anywhere else to go."

I grinned back. "Okay. I suppose I could stuff down one slice."

We drove to the Pizza Hut at the edge of town and parked at the back. It was nearly eleven, and cars were pulling out and heading back into town.

Colin held my hand while we walked to the entrance.

We went inside and ordered a couple of slices of cheese pizza and Cokes from a girl in my Spanish class who was waiting on tables.

"I've been wondering about you and Nikki," Colin said after the sodas had been served. "Mind if I ask why you're living with her?"

"She's my cousin. I'm just here for a semester."

He nodded and gazed at me with curiosity. "Just for fun?"

"No." I hadn't told anyone here why I was in Franklin Heights. It's embarrassing to admit your family is falling apart at the seams.

But Colin seemed trustworthy.

"My parents needed some time alone," I said, self-consciously picking up my Coke. "Things were getting a little rough between them."

His eyebrows rose.

"I don't mean violent," I said. "They just weren't getting along very well."

I sipped at my soda.

"Sorry." When I replaced the Coke on the table, he covered my hand with his. It was very warm.

"That's okay."

"So how do you like Franklin Heights?" he asked, leaning forward. He smiled. "The truth."

I hesitated. "It's"—I smiled back—"different. It's pretty small."

"This town's not the same as it used to be."

"How so?"

"You heard about Sean Wallace, right?"

"Yes. It's horrible."

"First, a fire is set in the hills and someone dies. Then Sean's killed. Things like that never used to happen here."

"It's really scary."

"Do you get along with Nikki?"

I didn't want to tell him the truth. I don't know why. Family loyalty, I guess.

"Sure."

He stared at me intently. "You know what I think? I think she's very immature and not very bright."

The scrutiny in his gaze made me feel uncomfortable. I gently pulled my hand away.

I shrugged. "She's hanging out with some people who've had a bad influence on her."

"That's for sure." He continued to stare at me. "Did I offend you? I mean, by telling you I don't like Nikki?"

"No. Sometimes she can be hard to like."

Our slices arrived.

"Have you and Eve started the article about Heath yet?" Colin asked.

I smiled, glad for the change in subject. "I'm having trouble getting started. We're going to talk to his parents. At least, we'll try. I'm hoping they will give us some good information about Heath that we can use."

"Good."

"I'm not sure anyone really has a sense about what Heath is . . . was really like," I said.

"I'm sure they don't. He was cipher around school. No one really noticed him."

The rest of our conversation was okay, but the warmth that Colin had shown me earlier was gone. I guessed he was embarrassed that I hadn't agreed with him about Nikki.

Actually, I couldn't have agreed more. I can't stand Nikki. But it seemed tacky to bad-mouth my own cousin, especially when I was staying in her home.

We finished our pizza and headed out to the parking lot. There were only four cars in the lot, and we strolled toward the Volvo at the back.

I stopped and grabbed Colin's arm. "Colin! Look at your dad's car!"

Colin's steps slowed. "What the—"

He ran to his car with me right behind him. We stopped and stared at the dark blue Volvo.

It had been sprayed with white paint. In big block letters, it said, JULIA IS A KILLER!

~10

"What is *this?*" Colin said over and over. "What the hell is *this?*"

He paced around his dad's car.

"Oh, Colin!" I said. "I'm so sorry this happened."

He turned to me. "What does this mean—'Julia is a killer'?"

I shook my head. "It's ridiculous. It doesn't make sense."

Colin kicked a stone out of the parking lot, swore, and paced some more.

"What's my dad going to say?" he said. "He loves this car!"

All I could do was pace with him and say I was sorry it happened. I was too humiliated to say any more. How could I explain?

After about fifteen minutes, he walked over to the pool of light under the overhead pole and checked his watch.

"I'd better get it over with," Colin said. "I'm going inside to call my dad."

"Better call the police, too," I said.

He nodded and left. In about five minutes he returned.

"Julia, my dad will be coming soon and so will the cops. My dad's going to blow his stack when he sees this. I called you a cab—"

"I don't mind waiting," I said. "I think I should be here when your dad arrives."

It was the *least* I could do.

"I don't think you'll want to be anywhere near my dad when he sees his car," Colin said.

"Okay," I said. "I'm...so sorry this happened."

"Just leave when the cab gets here. I hope it arrives before my dad does."

I rested my hand on his arm. "Colin, this is awful."

I felt terrible. Colin's father's car was ruined because of me.

I thought about how my dad would have reacted if his best car had been vandalized like this. He would have been breathing fire.

The cab arrived and I got in. I rode home, the pizza parking lot diminishing in the back window.

Great date, Julia, I told myself. *I'm sure Colin can't wait for another night out with you.*

"What's going to happen this time?" he'd probably say, coming to pick me up. "Somebody going to blow up the movie theater because you're inside?"

I knew there wouldn't be a next time.

I felt guilty leaving Colin back there to face his dad, but I was glad to get out of there before the police arrived. What would I have said? What *could* I have said without telling the whole story about the fire in the hills?

"Do you know anyone named Julia?" the officers would certainly ask.

I wondered if Colin would tell them who "Julia" is.

Would he protect me? Or would he tell? I'd better have something ready to say if the police show up at Aunt Helen's house.

The cab dropped me off at the curb, and I went inside the house.

Aunt Helen was sitting in the living room watching TV. She looked up. "Hi, Julia. Did you have a good time?"

"Great," I lied.

"Somebody named Eve Lenhart called," she said. "She wants you to call her back, even if it's late, she said."

"Okay."

I hurried upstairs and called Eve from the phone in my aunt and uncle's room.

"I'm so glad you called back," she said. "We have an interview tomorrow afternoon with Heath Quinn's dad. His mother has to work, so she won't be there."

"Okay," I said. I wasn't feeling enthusiastic about anything right now, but I was glad to get this news. Maybe I could finally learn something about Heath and where he might be. "What time and where?"

"Two o'clock at his house."

"Good."

"Why don't you make a list of questions you

want to ask," she said. "I will, too. Then let's meet at one o'clock at my house and go over them."

"Okay. I'll see you then."

"Julia?"

"Yeah?"

"Did you have a good time tonight? On your date with Colin?"

"Oh. Well, let's say I've had better dates in my life." I paused a second. "I don't really want to talk about it."

There was a short silence. "See you tomorrow."

"Bye."

We hung up and I headed toward my room. I noticed that Nikki's bedroom door was closed. She must be in bed already, I thought.

She'd slept most of the day. That wasn't like her. Seeing Heath at her window had seemed to have shocked the life out of her. Or maybe the sleeping pill from last night had left her groggy all day.

I went to my room and made a list of ten questions to ask Mr. Quinn. I figured I'd think of more as we talked to him.

The police hadn't shown up before I went to bed to ask about Colin's dad's car. Maybe they'd question me tomorrow. Or maybe Colin didn't say anything about me.

I felt so awful thinking about his father and that beautiful Volvo. I didn't look forward to facing Colin on Monday. I'd already said I was sorry several times, but all the apologies in the world wouldn't fix his dad's car.

What a mess. If only I'd never come here!

* * *

"Feel like talking now about your date with Colin?" Eve asked me the next day on the way to Heath's house in her car.

"Not really. But I don't expect him to ask me out again."

She looked over at me; there was relief in her eyes.

"I'm sure he decided I wasn't his type," I said.

Eve sighed. "I'm beginning to wonder who *is* his type."

"It was my fault," I said. "Really."

She nodded, but she didn't ask any more questions because we'd just pulled up in front of the Quinn home.

"Oh, there's—" she said.

I looked at the Quinn's house and I saw someone familiar—the guy who'd been at the park with the camera—walk around from the back of the house.

"Do you know him?" I asked her.

"Uh, no. I thought I did, but I was mistaken."

"He's the Mystery Man," I said. "But I'm going to find out once and for all who he is."

He peered around the garage toward the front door.

I got out of the car. "Hello," I called out to him.

He looked up abruptly and saw me. He froze a second, then bolted across the neighbor's yard.

"I just want to talk to you!"

He walked swiftly down the street and disappeared between two houses half-way down the block.

"I sure wish I knew who that guy is," I said.

"He probably had a good reason for being

87

there," Eve said. But she looked worried.

"So why did he run?"

"I don't know. Have you seen him before?"

"Twice. I wonder what he was doing in back of the Quinns' house?"

Eve didn't respond.

"Maybe Mr. Quinn can tell us that," I said. "Do you have your list of questions?"

"Yes."

We sat and looked up at the house. It was an old, two-story brick house on the edge of town. A dilapidated wooden porch clung to the front, its paint peeling and its stairs sagging.

"Ready?" I said.

"I'm nervous," Eve said.

"So'm I."

"Did you remember a pen?"

"In my bag." She fumbled through her bag and pulled out a ballpoint.

"Good. I hope he remembers we're coming."

We climbed the steps, and Eve tapped on the door.

We waited.

"Try again," I said.

She knocked a second time, harder, and the door slowly swung open.

Eve glanced at me, startled.

"The door wasn't closed." She turned back and called into the house. "Mr. Quinn?"

There was no answer.

"I hope he's all right," she said.

"Mr. Quinn?" I said loudly. "Are you home?"

No answer.

Nothing.

I pushed the door open a little further and leaned inside.

"Mr. Quinn?"

The house was dark and silent. I could see into the living room at the right. Drooping drapes were closed, and the room was filled with shadows.

"Maybe we should go in and make sure he's okay," Eve said.

I wondered if the Mystery Man had hurt Mr. Quinn. Why else would he have run when I called to him?

"Mr. Quinn *did* say we could come," Eve said.

I nodded and stepped inside. Eve followed close behind.

"Mr. Quinn?" We both called out his name this time.

The dining room was to the left. It was dark, too, with ratty shades pulled low.

"This place needs airing," Eve whispered, grimacing.

The house had a distinctive odor—a close, dusty smell, as if the windows hadn't been opened in years.

We walked through the dining room, the dark wooden floorboards creaking, and into the kitchen.

"Mr. Quinn?"

"Julia, look," Eve said. "The kitchen door is open."

The door with four dirty panes of glass was standing open. The skeleton key sat in its place in the lock.

"What do you want to bet that the Mystery Man

was in here?" I said. "It wasn't locked."

"You think he just walked in?"

"*We* did."

I looked around the kitchen. A half-dozen plates sat on the counter next to the sink, and the water dripped every few seconds from the faucet.

I walked over the chipped linoleum floor and pushed on the faucet handle. It didn't budge, and the drip continued.

"Needs a new washer," I said.

"I'll be sure to tell Mr. Quinn you said so," Eve said, smiling a little.

I grinned back at her.

"This is weird," Eve said. "Mr. Quinn said he'd be here."

"Maybe he had too much to drink and fell asleep upstairs," I said.

"That's what I was thinking," Eve said. "I hope he's all right."

"You think we should check upstairs?"

"This is scary enough. I don't want to go any further. You think we could be charged with trespassing?" she said.

"We were invited," I said, shrugging, "and we found the door open."

"This is so weird," she repeated.

"Think we should have the police check?" I said. "If that guy hurt him—"

"No, I don't want to call the police," Eve said. "If everything's okay, Mr. Quinn might be furious when the cops show up."

In spite of being scared, I wanted to go upstairs. First, I wanted to make sure Heath's father was okay, but I also wanted to learn something—anything—about Heath that might help us find him.

"I'd like to see Heath's room," I said.

Eve's eyes got big. She swallowed.

"I don't know."

"I'll go up myself if you don't want to go with me," I said.

"No—you shouldn't go up alone," Eve said. "What if his dad's up there?"

"If he's up there, why didn't he answer when we called?"

"Maybe he's hurt or drunk."

"Or dead," I said. "We'd better check on him."

"You're pretty cool," she said.

"Are you kidding? I'm trembling all over."

We walked back through the dining room. This time I noticed the table. It was old—a chrome and formica job that would have been more appropriate in a big, eat-in kitchen in the 1950s.

We came out of the dining room and stood at the bottom of the steps in the foyer. The stairs rose before us into the gloom on the second floor.

"After you," Eve said.

I smiled wryly and started up the stairs.

"Mr. Quinn?" I called. "Mr. Quinn?"

No answer, of course.

I was hoping that if he'd fallen asleep, he'd wake up and realize we were here.

The stairs squeaked loudly under our feet.

The second floor was darker than the one we'd just left. Four doors opened into the hall that stretched from the front to the back of the house.

I pointed to the first room on the right at the top of the stairs. Eve nodded.

We tiptoed to the doorway and looked in.

It was the bathroom. It didn't look as if it had been cleaned in a very long time.

Across the hall was another room. It was a storage room, filled with junk. An old vacuum cleaner stood in the center; a dusty, cracked mirror in an ancient wooden frame leaned against a cardboard box; several scratched metal chairs stood around the room looking like tired aluminum sentries. We moved on.

We stopped at the doorway to the room at the back of the house. Eve gasped and grabbed my arm.

A bed stood in the shadows next to the far wall. On top of the bed lay a man, his arms spread out at his sides.

11

"Is he dead?" Eve whispered.

As if in answer, a loud snore came from the prostrate man on the bed.

I spotted the whiskey bottle on the floor and pointed at it.

"He's passed out."

"Let's get out of here," Eve said.

"I want to see Heath's room."

"Are you crazy? Mr. Quinn might wake up!"

"Just a quick peek," I said.

She rolled her eyes but followed me across the hall to the only room we hadn't seen yet.

Its door was closed. I grasped the doorknob and pushed it open. We stepped into a small room. As in the rest of the rooms, the shades were pulled down and the room was filled with shadows.

A single bed was pushed up against the wall. There was no bedspread or pillow on it, only a thin blanket. A banged-up wooden desk sat next to the opposite wall. Posters for heavy metal and rap groups were tacked up on three sides, and two bookshelves lined the fourth wall. Papers and clothes were strewn around the room on the bed, desk, and floor.

Eve followed me to the bookshelf, and we read the paperback spines. They were mostly adventure novels for young boys. It looked as if Heath had stopped reading a long time ago.

I glanced down at his desk. A receipt from Petie's, a convenience store down the street, lay on the desk.

I looked at it more closely.

It was dated September 15. *That was three days after the fire!*

"Eve, look at this," I whispered.

She stepped up behind me.

"What is it?"

"Look at the date."

"The fifteenth. Does that mean something?

"The fire was on the twelfth."

"So?"

"Heath bought stuff at Petie's three days after the fire."

"What do you mean? Heath's dead. His father must've bought stuff at Petie's."

"Why would the receipt be in here?" I said.

"Because his dad put it down when he was in here," Eve said.

I slipped the receipt in my pocket. "Ready to leave?" I said.

"Ten minutes ago!"

We hurried down the stairs and out the front door, closing the front door firmly behind us.

* * *

"Eve, Heath is alive," I said.

Eve and I had decided to stop for a Coke before she drove me home. I sat opposite her at a table at Hardee's.

Eve looked up from her soda. "Julia, that receipt isn't proof that Heath is alive."

"I know."

Should I tell her what I know? I couldn't decide. Maybe I could tell her part of it and see how she reacted.

"Nikki is sure she saw him last night."

"Where?"

"Near the house."

"That seems pretty unlikely," she said. "She probably saw someone else."

"We've also heard from him."

"What do you mean?"

"Threatening notes."

"From *Heath?*"

"I know it sounds crazy," I said. "But I think he's still alive. Someone else died in that fire."

She stared at me. "How do you know Heath wrote the notes?"

"I checked the typing in the notes with a paper he turned in at school a week before he disappeared. It was written on the same typewriter." I hit myself on the side of the head. "I should have looked for that old typewriter when we were in Heath's house!" I sighed heavily. "I'm such an idiot. Do you remember seeing a typewriter?"

"No."

"Neither do I."

"I can't believe he's *writing* to you! What kind of threatening notes?"

I didn't say anything for a moment. How far should I go here? I couldn't tell her everything. Or could I? What would she do with that information? Would she go to the police? Or would she help me find Heath so that I could talk to him?

"He . . . he says he's going to kill me."

"Kill you!"

I nodded.

"Why would he want to kill you?"

I nervously took a sip from my straw, then sat back in the booth.

"I was with some people who set fire to that cabin in the hills."

"What!" Eve leaned forward in her seat. "Who were you with?"

"I'd rather not say."

"Oh, you don't have to," she said. "I can guess. Nikki and Matt. That's just like something they'd do for fun."

"It's a terrible mess."

"I can see that."

"I wanted to go to the police," I said, "but Nikki threatened to tell them that the whole thing was my idea. She said the others would back her up."

"I'm sure they would have."

"Sean was there, too."

"And Sean was murdered!"

"I was waiting for you to bring that up," I said.

"I hardly knew Sean. And I was so interested in hearing about your date with Colin and nervous about talking to Mr. Quinn, I didn't think about it at the time." She frowned. "So you think Heath murdered Sean?"

I nodded. "For revenge. I think he means to kill everyone who was in the hills that night."

"I wonder where Heath is living?" she said. "Do you think he's staying at home?"

"I doubt it. I bet he's hiding out somewhere. But he's been home since the fire if that receipt was his."

"Could I see it again?"

I pulled the paper from my pocket and handed it to her.

She looked at it and nodded. "Petie's receipts list the purchased items. Look at the things he bought."

She handed it back and I read the list: canned beans, canned ravioli, flashlight, dried apricots, sodas, batteries, crackers, can opener.

"Stuff that doesn't need refrigerating," I said. "Camping stuff."

"I wonder where he got the money to buy it?"

"That wouldn't be hard," I said. "Just stop by when his dad's passed out and his mom is at work, and take the money from his wallet."

"You know, this still could be Mr. Quinn's receipt."

"There's one way to find out."

"How?"

"Let's go get your yearbook, then go to Petie's and ask the clerk if this guy came in to buy supplies last week."

"Heath's face has been plastered on the front

page of the paper and TV," Eve said. "I mean, do we really need the yearbook? Wouldn't the clerk know if he'd come in?"

"*I* probably wouldn't," I said. "I don't remember faces that well, and if I thought someone was dead, I wouldn't be looking for him. Does the receipt say the time of purchase?"

I looked at the slip of paper. "Three-fourteen."

"Three fourteen in the morning," Eve said. "He went in during the graveyard shift."

"We could stop by Petie's around midnight and see if the clerk recognizes the picture of Heath."

"Let's do it," she said. "I'll pick you up at twelve tonight."

"How am I going to get out at midnight without getting asked a lot of questions?"

"Want me to do it myself?" she asked. "I don't mind."

"No. We're writing the article together, and I'm up to my neck in . . . whatever happened to Heath. I'll be ready at twelve, but don't ring the bell. I'll try to be on the front porch, waiting."

Aunt Helen and Uncle Jim usually went to bed sometime between 10:30 and 11:30. Nikki had spent the weekend in her room and was still there.

I tried to study. By 11:00, I hadn't heard my aunt and uncle go to their bedroom, and I was getting nervous.

I tiptoed to the top of the stairs and listened.

They were watching an old movie on TV. I could hear corny music and tap dancing.

Mom and I used to watch old musicals together.

But that was back in my other life. The life where there was no arson or murder. Just schoolwork, dances, and dates on the weekends.

I wondered if I'd ever get back to that life.

I went back to my room and watched the clock. Maybe I could sneak downstairs, go out the kitchen door without being seen, and wait on the front porch.

But I knew that wouldn't work. They'd see me even if I tiptoed down the stairs.

Finally, at 11:47, I heard them trudging up the stairs. I sat, frozen in my chair, till I heard them close their door.

I pulled a jacket from my closet, shrugged it on, and very quietly went downstairs and slipped out the front door.

Except for the streetlight shining above the road, the night was dark. The moon and stars were shrouded behind thick clouds. I shivered in the chill.

I figured it was about eleven-fifty. Ten minutes to wait.

I sat on the stoop between large shrubs and looked up the street. The houses are far apart on Wylder Road, and the street looked gloomy.

The night was quiet; not even the crickets were chirping.

A block away, headlights pierced the night; a van was approaching.

A half-block away, it decreased its speed and snapped the headlights out.

Just before it was even with our house, it pulled up next to the curb across the street and stopped.

I wondered if the driver could see me. I didn't think so. The streetlight's beams didn't reach this far, and I sat between two bushes that thrust shadows around them.

I sat frozen and watched the van. I couldn't tell the make or color because it was too far from the streetlight.

Nothing happened. It just sat there.

I squinted at it. Could it be Eve? When we'd gone to Heath's house, she'd driven a blue sedan. Was this van her family's second car? Was she being overcautious, cutting off her lights so my aunt and uncle wouldn't see me leave?

It was too dark to see my watch. It had to be pretty close to midnight. Maybe it *was* Eve. Maybe she had arrived a little early and was waiting for me.

I had just decided to wait a few more minutes when a car approached from the opposite direction. It pulled right up to the curb in front of the house.

Eve.

I rushed down the front walk and scrambled into her car.

"Hi," she said.

"Someone's watching the house from that van over there."

She looked. "Oh, no." She looked at me. "Do you know who it is?"

"I don't know," I said. "Maybe Heath. Where would he have gotten a van?"

"I guess he could've stolen it."

"It might also belong to his dad," I said. "Let's get out of here."

Eve pulled away from the curb. "I have my yearbook."

"Good."

We slowly passed the van sitting at the curb. The driver turned his head so we couldn't see his face.

"Did you see who it was?" I asked.

"No, did you?"

"No. Let's see if he follows us."

"Julia, that has to be Heath. Who else could it be?"

"I don't know," I said. "Unless Matt or Randy is following us."

I looked back over my shoulder at the dark form sitting across from the house. The front and taillights bloomed and the van turned around, using a driveway next door.

"Here he comes," I said. "He's following."

"What's he *doing* here?" Eve muttered between her teeth.

She drove down to Mt. Vernon Road, a main artery through town, and turned right. Petie's was just a few blocks away.

She pulled into the brightly lit parking lot and stopped next to the door.

"Can't get any closer than this," she said. She looked back over her shoulder.

"Is he still back there?" I asked.

"Yes," she said.

"Let's see if he pulls into the lot."

The van sped up and roared past the store, the driver shielding his face.

"Recognize the van?" I asked Eve. "It was a cinnamon color and looked pretty old."

"No," she said. She looked more irritated than worried.

We got out of the car. Eve looked over her shoulder for the van, but it was gone. I pulled open the heavy door to Petie's.

Except for the clerk standing behind the counter, the store was empty.

"Hi," I said to the clerk.

He mumbled "Hi" and moved to the cash register. The name *Tim* was stitched in red thread on his pocket.

"Hi," Eve said. "We don't need to buy anything." She opened her yearbook to the place that was marked with a paper clip. "We're looking for a guy who might have been in here last week. Do you work through the night hours?"

Tim nodded. "Eleven to seven."

"Great," Eve said. She pointed to Heath's picture. "Do you remember seeing him in here last week? It would've been around three A.M."

Tim looked at the picture. "Uh, yeah," he said. "That might have been him, but I'm not sure. I remember that greased-back hair. He bought stuff that you'd use camping. I think I asked him if he was getting camping supplies."

"What did he say?" I asked.

"He said, 'Yeah.'" Tim looked back and forth between us. "How come you're looking for him? This guy do something wrong?"

I had to wonder why Tim hadn't recognized Heath's picture which had been plastered over the news for several nights.

"Have you, by any chance, been on vacation lately?" I asked him.

He grinned. "How'd you know? The tan, right?"

"That's it." I grinned back. He did have a dark tan for late September. "It's been fairly cool here the last couple of weeks. Where'd you go?"

"L.A. Did lots of roller-blading."

"Sounds like fun."

"Well," Eve said, closing her yearbook. "Thanks a lot."

"Hope you find your man," he said.

"Thanks," I said.

"Want me to tell him you're looking for him if he comes in again?"

"Uh, yeah," I said. "Tell him Julia would like to talk to him."

Tim saluted. "Have a good night."

We headed for the door. Eve put a hand on my arm. "Do you see him out there?"

I looked.

"I don't see anyone," I said.

"Let's go."

We hurried out to the car and opened the doors. Eve hadn't locked them. I quickly checked the backseat. Empty. We hustled into the car.

"Well, the clerk *thought* it was Heath," I said.

"So, it certainly wasn't Heath's father who came in to buy those supplies," Eve said.

"Heath *must* have bought them!"

"I can't believe he's alive," Eve said. She turned to look at me. "So who died in the fire?"

"I don't know. That night in the hills, we saw a

hobo walking in the same direction. Matt threw rocks at him and he ran on ahead of us. It could have been that guy."

"That sounds like something Matt would do," Eve said. "He's such a jerk."

She started the engine and pulled out of the lot.

"Anybody following us?" she asked.

"No."

"Good."

Eve drove me to Nikki's house. We pulled up at the curb, and I pulled my key out of my pocket.

"I'll wait till you're inside," Eve said.

"Thanks. Be careful driving home."

"Hey, I don't have to worry. I wasn't in the hills with you guys."

"I wish I hadn't been there!"

I ran to the front stoop, opened the door, waved to Eve, and let myself inside.

Locking the door behind me, I tiptoed up the stairs.

The door across the hall was yanked open.

"Julia!" Aunt Helen, wearing her robe over a nightgown, stood in her bedroom doorway.

"Oh, hi, Aunt Helen." What was she doing up so late?

"Julia, where were you? We were worried about you!"

"I'm sorry. I went out for a little while with Eve Lenhart. We're working on a story for the school paper."

Aunt Helen sighed heavily, a frown still creasing her forehead.

"I didn't know what to think, with a murderer loose."

"I really am sorry."

"There was a call for you. We came in to tell you, but you weren't there."

"A call came in this late?"

"Yes. A boy named Heath." She paused, then asked, "Isn't that the name of the boy who's missing?"

12

"*Heath?*" I asked. "Are you sure that's what he said?"

"Yes," Aunt Helen said. "I was so surprised, I asked him to repeat it. He definitely said Heath."

"But he didn't give a last name?"

"No. Do you know more than one Heath?"

I blinked. "I guess I must," I said. "Did he leave a number?"

"No."

Of course not.

"Did he say he'd call back?"

"He said he'd call tomorrow."

I nodded. "Thanks, Aunt Helen. And I'm sorry I scared you."

"Yes, well, please don't go out again this late."

"I won't."

I closed my bedroom door and sat on the bed.

Heath had called!

What could he want?

I was both relieved and nervous. I wouldn't have to spend time looking for him anymore. But if I arranged to meet him, was I providing an opportunity for him to kill me?

If it really was Heath who had called, how could he have been in the van that followed us?

He could have stopped at a public phone and called just after roaring off down the road past Petie's. He would have known I wouldn't be home to take the call.

Why would he have called if he knew I wouldn't be there?

I wished I'd asked Aunt Helen what time he'd called. Then I'd have a better idea whether it was the same person who'd followed us.

I got ready for bed and slid under the covers. My head was so filled with questions, it took nearly two hours to get to sleep.

I couldn't wait to talk to Eve about it tomorrow.

Nikki didn't mention Heath's phone call the next morning. She must not have been awake when the call came in. She had been oddly quiet since she'd thought she'd seen Heath at her window. She hadn't been going out with Matt or with her other friends, and she spent most of her time in her room. When she'd come downstairs, she'd walked around the house several times to see that every door and window was locked.

She drove us, as usual, to school.

"What's new with Matt?" I asked her.

"I haven't seen him," she said.

"What about Brandi and Randy?"

"I don't know."

She didn't offer more, and I didn't press. For some reason, she was isolating herself from other people. It must be fear, I thought. And maybe depression over Sean's death.

I caught up with Eve in the hall before classes and whispered the news about the midnight phone call.

"He *called* you?" Eve said.

"Whoever called said his name was Heath. I don't know any other Heath."

"And he said he'd call back?"

"I suppose he means after school. I'll go right home and wait. I hope he calls."

"Me, too! But it's scary."

"I wonder what he'll say?"

"Maybe he'll rant and rave about the justice of revenge. Remember that day in lit class?"

"Yes," I said. "I keep thinking about it."

"Should I tell Colin about it?" Eve asked.

At the mention of Colin's name, my stomach tightened. What was I going to say when I saw him? How many times could I apologize for what had happened to his dad's car? If I had a job, I could offer to pay to get it repainted. But I didn't have a penny to my name. And I couldn't ask Mom and Dad for it, not with all the trouble between them.

It was one more thing to feel guilty about.

"Tell him there's a possibility that Heath's still alive, and we're checking on it," I said.

"He'll be curious."

"Just tell him that we're doing a lot of investigating and the article is moving along. Maybe his heart will soften toward me a little."

Eve smiled wryly. "But we haven't even started writing it yet."

"We will. We just need more information. I thought we'd get some good stuff from his dad."

"I'll tell Colin that no one came to the door when we went to interview Mr. Quinn."

"Okay."

"Call me right after you talk to Heath!" Eve said.

"*If* he calls back."

I rushed home right after school and waited. And waited.

Heath didn't call.

I waited all evening and nothing happened. I stayed up until 12:30, hoping he'd call as late as he had the night before, but still no call came in.

The next day I pulled Eve aside before lit class.

"Heath didn't call," I said. "But I have an idea. Will you come over to my aunt's house tonight after dinner?"

"Sure. What's up?"

"Well, if Heath is alive and writing the notes and calling me, he's got to be living somewhere around here."

"That makes sense."

"I bet he's staying in his own home. We found the receipt there. And if his father is often drunk, and his mom is away from the house a lot, they wouldn't even know he was there."

Eve looked at me, thoughtfully. "That's possible, I suppose. But what about the supplies he bought from Petie's?"

"I don't know," I said. "That's a good question."

"He wouldn't need camping supplies to stay in his own home."

"True. I may be wrong about this, Eve. It could be a waste of time. But I have a hunch that if we watch the house for a couple of days, we might see him coming and going."

"A stakeout?"

"Right. Could we use your car?"

"Sure."

"So I'll see you tonight?"

"Right. How about seven?"

"Great," I said.

"So what do we do if we see him?" Eve said after we pulled up across the street from the Quinn's house later that night.

"I've been thinking about that," I said. "I think you should stay in the car. I'll call his name and say we want to talk with him."

"He'll wonder if we're going to turn him in to the police," Eve said.

"I'll tell him we only want to talk, and I'll walk toward him with my hands in the air so he sees that I don't have a weapon."

"So he can blow you away?"

"I don't think that'll happen."

"You're willing to bet your life on that?"

"He had the opportunity to kill me on Friday night." I told her about the gun at the concession stand window. "I don't know for sure if it was

Heath, but I saw a flash of that beige jacket he always wears."

Eve shook her head. "None of this makes sense. Why would he kill the others and spare you? Heath is an angry guy, but he doesn't seem capable of murder."

I turned to her, surprised. "Did you know him very well?"

"Oh, no," she said quickly. "He just doesn't seem like the murdering type."

We stared across the street at the Quinn home. The sun was sitting low in the Western sky and glinting off the front windows. From where we sat, we could see the front and one side of the house.

As before, the drapes were pulled shut, and it looked quiet.

"This could be a long wait," Eve said, "so I brought some bagels and lemonade."

I grinned at her. "You think Sherlock Holmes had it this good?"

She laughed and passed me the sack of bagels and poured lemonade from a thermos into a paper cup.

"You think you'll ever tell me why your date with Colin was so bad?" she asked.

I sighed. "I'm embarrassed. Could we talk about it later? Just thinking of it makes me feel terrible."

"You're not just making that up?" she said. "I mean, because you know how much I like him?"

"Believe me, I'm not. It was a disastrous date."

"Okay. I mentioned you today, and his face didn't change."

"I'm surprised he didn't scream."

"You've made me very curious."

"Okay." I sighed heavily. "Someone wrecked his dad's car. We came out of the Pizza Hut and someone had spray-painted 'Julia is a killer!' all over the car."

"Oh, no!"

"It *had* to have been Heath. But of course, I couldn't explain it to Colin. I stood there and babbled and apologized for what had happened and claimed that I didn't know who would do such a thing. I felt like such a low-life!"

"I can see why."

"Thank you."

"I'm sorry," Eve said. "I meant, that must have been awful for you!"

I still had the feeling this was *good* news to her and not bad.

"It was horrible."

We ate in silence and watched the darkness grow deep around us.

"What do cops do to pass the time?" I wondered aloud. "This could get pretty boring."

"What time is it?"

I checked my watch. "Almost eight-thirty."

By 9:00 we'd eaten all the bagels.

"As I said, this could be a waste of time."

"You mean, especially now that the bagels are gone?" Eve said.

"Right."

Another hour passed, and Eve, leaning back in the driver's seat, snored softly.

I was beginning to think it was time to give up and go home to bed when a movement in the shadows near the house caught my eye. I sat up and stared into the darkness.

There it was again. Someone emerged from the deep shadows, limping, and stood under a tall tree next to the house.

"Eve—somebody's standing next to the tree across the street."

Eve woke up, startled. "What? Where?"

The dark figure jumped up and grabbed hold of the lowest branch, then pulled himself into the tree.

"What's he doing?" I said.

We watched the figure slowly climb two-thirds of the way up the tree and step awkwardly over to the Quinns' roof. He steadied himself for a moment, then lay on his stomach with his top half looking over the edge. He grabbed hold of a window into the attic and pulled himself inside.

"That was Heath, wasn't it?" I said.
"That was Heath," Eve said.

13

"He's living in his own attic," I said. "That's why he needed to buy 'camping' supplies."

"His parents probably don't even know he's there," Eve said.

We sat in the car and watched the attic window. A dim light came from there now, probably from the flashlight Heath had bought at Petie's.

"I want to talk to him," I said. "I've been waiting to see him for a long time."

"What are you going to do?"

"I'm going to try and get into the attic the way Heath did."

"Now?"

I turned to her. "Eve, I have to. I've had a hard time living with myself since that night in the hills. I didn't do enough to stop them from setting the fire. Now I have a second chance to help Heath. I think he might listen to me. He could've killed me the other day in the park, but he didn't."

"Okay, but if you're going, so am I."

"You don't have to, Eve," I said.

"I know, but I want to."

We both left the car and walked across the street to the tree.

"He's taller than we are," Eve whispered. "I can't jump up to that first branch."

I looked around me for something to stand on. I remembered how Heath had used the garbage can when he climbed onto Nikki's garage roof.

"Maybe there's a garbage can around in the back," I said softly.

"Wait, I have a penlight on my key chain," Eve said.

I heard a jangle of keys, then a tiny light appeared in her hand. It didn't do much to illuminate the yard, but it helped us see the path directly ahead of us as we headed around to the backyard.

We found a beat-up garbage can behind the garage and dragged it to the tree.

"That's better," I said.

I stood up on it and easily reached the first branch. I pulled myself up and then climbed up to the next branch and the next. Eve followed close behind.

The roof was only about two feet away from a thick limb, so it was easy to step onto the gently sloping surface.

I wondered if Heath could have seen us climbing the tree next to the attic window, and whether he was waiting for us inside.

As Heath had done earlier, I lay on my stomach over the edge of the roof. For the first time, I looked down at the dark, murky ground below which was barely visible in the gloomy night. It would be a long fall if I couldn't reach the attic window.

The screenless window stood open. From my position on the roof, I couldn't see more than a few feet into the attic. The small light that we'd seen from the ground wasn't there now.

I pictured Heath sitting in a dark corner waiting for us, and for a moment, I nearly changed my mind.

"You okay?" Eve whispered.

"Yeah."

"You going ahead?"

I paused only a second. "Yeah."

I scooted down so more of my body hung over the roof, and Eve grabbed my legs from behind.

If there had been a light on in the attic, I would've been able to see it now. But all that was there was the blackness of the room.

I grabbed hold of the window frame and pulled.

"You want me to let go?" Eve asked.

"Yes," I said softly to her.

She released my legs and I jerked myself hard into the window. I rolled in a somersault, banging the back of my head and shoulders on the hard, wooden floor of the attic.

I leaped to my feet, taking a defensive pose, expecting to be grabbed or shoved.

Nothing happened.

"Heath?"

I'd wished I'd taken the penlight from Eve. I couldn't see anything.

"Heath, I only want to talk to you. Are you here?"

There was only silence in the room. Then I heard Eve's voice.

"Julia, are you okay?"

I turned to the window and called up. "Yeah. Come on, I'll help you."

In a half-minute, she landed with a thud next to me, but not on her head because I was able to guide her body in the fall.

"Is he here?" she asked, scrambling to her feet.

"I don't think so."

"Where did he go?"

"I don't know. You still have your penlight?"

I heard her pull keys out of her pocket, and she handed me the tiny flashlight. I turned it on and shined it around the room.

"Look at this!" Eve murmured.

The attic room had been outfitted like a campsite. A bedspread lay on the floor. On top of that was a sleeping bag, a pillow, and the grocery items that had been listed on Petie's receipt, including the flashlight.

"And here's the typewriter," I said.

A manual typewriter, looking more than fifty years old, sat at the edge of the bedspread.

"What do you want to bet the Ts and Es don't type clearly?" I pushed my hand into my pocket and came up with a piece of scrap paper. I slid it into the typewriter and hit the *T*, then the *E*.

"What'd I tell you." I showed her the paper.

She nodded, then looked above her. "Julia, look at the ceiling!"

The long, sloping ceiling was papered with the *Franklin Heights Courier* articles about the fire in the hills, the discovery of the body, and the disappearance of Heath Quinn.

And the murder of Sean Wallace.

"Wow."

I shone the light deeper into the attic room and found the stairs leading down to the second floor.

"He must be downstairs."

"I wonder why he came in through the attic window?"

"Maybe he wanted to make sure his parents weren't home before coming in."

Eve looked at me. "So what do we do now?"

"We go to the police," I said, "before he kills anyone else."

"You're going to do *what*?" Nikki said. It was the most life I'd seen in her eyes in over a week.

I'd just gotten home. Eve and I had climbed out of the attic window the way we'd entered, helping each other climb onto the roof.

It was now about 11:00 P.M., and I found Nikki in her room listening to CDs. I told her what Eve and I had found in Heath's attic, and how the articles about the fire and Sean's death were plastered all over the ceilings.

"It's time," I said, standing next to the closed door. "We've got to tell the police what happened before he kills again."

"No way!" she said, her voice climbing higher in pitch. "You'll get us all sent to jail!"

"Would you rather die?"

"*Yes*!" she screamed. "I'd rather *die* than go to jail!"

"Nikki, that doesn't make any sense. Besides, Heath is alive, so you wouldn't be charged with murder. In fact, you didn't even set the fire!"

"But Matt did! He'll be charged with arson."

"If we tell the police, we can stop Heath from killing anyone else!"

"All we need is a gun to do that! We can protect ourselves!"

"Nikki, if Heath wants to kill you, he'll find a way, no matter how many guns you own. The only way we can stop him is to—"

"Kill him!" Nikki said. "Let's go to his attic and kill him!"

I stopped and stared at her. "You're around the bend, you know that? Tomorrow I'm going to the police. You can tell them whatever you want."

I turned and walked back to my bedroom.

The doorbell rang. I sighed. It was 11:00. What now?

I opened my door and went to the top of the stairs.

Below, Uncle Jim went to the front door.

"Yes?" he said.

"I'm Detective Harley with the Franklin Heights police department." I could only see him from the chest down. His hand reached into his breast pocket of his coat and produced a badge that he showed my uncle. "I'd like to talk with Nikki Stott. She your daughter?"

"Yes," Uncle Jim's voice went hoarse. He turned and called, "Nikki? Will you come down, please?"

He turned to the officer.

"What's happened? Is Nikki in some kind of trouble?"

"There's been another murder," the officer said. He consulted a small notebook. "A Matt Gifford. I understand he's a friend of your daughter's."

~14

"Matt!" Nikki shrieked, running down the stairs. *"Matt's dead?"*

Nikki knew even before the detective had told her. Harley was immediately interested.

"You knew about Gifford's death?" he asked.

Nikki realized what she'd said and quit sobbing. "I...I...I just assumed after Sean's murder..."

Aunt Helen, dressed in her bathrobe and nightgown, had come downstairs right behind Nikki. Now, white-faced and trembling, she invited Detective Harley to come into the living room and sit down.

"How did it happen?" Uncle Jim asked anxiously.

"He was shot," Harley said. "Once in the head."

Nikki cried out again and buried her face in her hands.

"Miss Stott—Nikki," Harley said. "I know this must be very difficult for you. But since you're a good friend of his, I'll have to ask you some questions."

"Go ahead," my uncle said.

Nikki stopped crying and sniffed loudly. Aunt Helen pulled a tissue from her pocket and handed it to her.

"When was the last time you saw Gifford?" Harley asked.

"Oh, uh," she glanced worriedly at me, and Harley followed her gaze with his eyes. "I think it was maybe yesterday."

"You didn't see him in school today?"

"Oh. Maybe it was today." She rubbed her forehead. "I can't really remember."

"You were Gifford's girlfriend, is that right?" the detective asked.

"Yes."

"Did he have any enemies that you know of?"

Nikki looked straight at me, her eyes wide with fear. Harley turned to look at me again.

"You a sister?" he asked. He took out a pen and clicked the point out.

"No, I'm Nikki's cousin," I said. "I'm here for a semester."

"What's your name?"

"Julia Bliss."

Harley grunted and wrote in his notebook. "I'll ask both of you, then. Are you aware of any enemies that Gifford might have had?"

Nikki quickly said, "No! Everyone liked Matt."

Harley looked at me. "What do you say, Julia? Did he have any enemies?"

"I told you," Nikki cried. "He didn't have enemies! Everybody—"

"I'd like to hear what Julia has to say," Harley said. "Hmmm?"

Everyone looked at me.

"He did have one enemy," I said. I think I sounded calm, but my heart was thudding loudly.

Nikki cried out and sobbed.

"Who's that?"

"Heath Quinn."

Harley frowned. "The kid that's missing?"

"Yes."

"What would Quinn have to do with Matt Gifford?"

"I swear, Julia, if you *tell*—!"

I gazed at Nikki. "Matt's dead," I said to her. "You don't have to protect him now."

I looked back at the detective. "Matt set fire to the cabin in the hills."

Harley's eyes opened wide and he sat up a little straighter.

"What?" Aunt Helen said. "Julia, what are you saying?"

"Matt, Nikki, Sean, Brandi, Randy, and I were in the hills that night."

Detective Harley scratched his face. "Would Sean be Sean Wallace, the football player who was killed a few days ago?"

"Yes."

"Oh, this is terrible!" Aunt Helen cried.

"Give me the last names of Brandi and Randy."

"Brandi Rivers and Randy Shaw."

"I hate you, Julia!" Nikki said between sobs.

Aunt Helen looked back and forth between Nikki

and me with a crushed, helpless expression on her face.

"Tell me what happened," Harley said. "Tell me everything."

So I described what happened in the hills that night. Then I told him about the threatening notes signed by Heath and how Heath had appeared at Nikki's window. Last, I told him about discovering Heath's hiding place in the Quinn's attic.

"We'll get over there tonight," Harley said, still scribbling in his notebook. He looked back up at me. "You want to add anything?"

"No," I said. "I've told you everything I know."

"I hope you feel good about what you've done," Nikki said caustically.

Aunt Helen and Uncle Jim looked stricken.

"I had no idea all this was going on," Aunt Helen murmured. "No idea."

Harley got up and tucked his notebook into his pocket. "Thanks, folks. Sorry to have to deliver tragic news, and I'm sorry to disturb you so late." He looked at me. "I appreciate your cooperation, Julia. We'll need to talk to you and Nikki again in the next few days."

I nodded. Harley left, and Uncle Jim closed the door behind him. He turned to us.

"I don't know what to say," he said after a moment. "How could my daughter be involved in something so serious without my knowing?"

Nikki didn't speak. She folded her arms and stared at the floor.

"What's happened to you, Nikki?" he asked. "I

don't think I even know you anymore."

Nikki sobbed, bolted up the stairs and slammed her bedroom door shut.

Aunt Helen turned to me. "We took you into our home because your mother and father needed help." Her face was white and stone-hard, her voice tight and angry. "And this is how you pay us back?"

"Helen..." Uncle Jim said.

"No, Jim, I'll have my say." Aunt Helen turned back to me. "Nikki was never a bad girl until you showed up. She'd always been happy and carefree; since you arrived, she's turned into a depressed, angry person. And now you implicate her in that fire. Is that how you repay a kindness, Julia? Is that how you tell us thank you?"

"This isn't Julia's fault," Uncle Jim said. "Helen, you're not being fair."

I didn't know what to say. Aunt Helen was right: I certainly had implicated Nikki in the arson and the death of whoever was inside the cabin. She hadn't set the fire, but she also hadn't tried to stop Matt and the others from setting it.

But how could I have told the detective only part of the story?

Uncle Jim, standing behind Aunt Helen, rested his hand on her shoulder. "Nikki's a big girl," he said quietly. "She makes her own decisions."

Aunt Helen turned, blinking away tears and hurried up the stairs.

Uncle Jim sighed. "I think we'd all better get to bed," he said. "It's late."

"Okay."

I climbed the steps behind him feeling a heavier sadness than I'd ever felt in my life. I went into my room and closed the door behind me.

Murder was the subject of everyone's conversations at school the next day. First, Sean had been shot, and now Matt. Who would be next?

And who could the murderer be? It could be anybody in Franklin Heights, everyone said. Anybody who knew both of the guys. Anybody who might have been jealous of their popularity or their talent on the football field.

No one suggested that it might be someone on whom they had inflicted their cruelty.

No one made a connection between Heath Quinn's disappearance and the deaths of the two jocks, but it was just a matter of time before they found out.

"What do you think will happen to Nikki?" Eve asked. I'd told her about last night's visit from Detective Harley.

"I don't know," I said. "She and I were both accessories to the crime, but we didn't actually set the fire. And we can't be sure that whoever died in the cabin wasn't already dead when the fire was set."

"That reminds me," Eve said. "Are you going to *The Bugle* meeting tonight?"

"Yes," I said. I had to face Colin sometime. "When does Colin expect to see our article?"

She winced. "This week. I'll have to tell him we'll write it for another issue."

"I don't think this is a good time to write an article about Heath," I said.

"I agree." She smiled. "See you at the meeting."

I didn't want to see Colin or go to the meeting, but I had to. I'd disappointed Colin twice: once on our date and again for not getting the article written for *The Bugle*. It was time to level with him about everything.

Maybe he wouldn't hate me so much.

I sat through the meeting after school and watched Colin's eyes. He looked at me once; after that, he didn't even glance my way.

After the meeting, I told Eve I was going to hang around and talk to Colin. She looked alarmed.

"I have to explain things to Colin," I said.

"You're going to tell him everything?"

"Yes. I trust him not to blab about it. After what happened to his dad's Volvo, I think he deserves to know."

"His dad has a Volvo?"

"It used to be beautiful."

"That's funny. I didn't think his parents had that kind of money."

I shrugged. "Don't worry, Eve. He isn't interested in me; I just don't want him to hate me so much."

"Okay," she said. "See you tomorrow."

She left the journalism classroom. There were only a couple of people left. Colin moved around the room, straightening the chairs and picking up stray pieces of paper.

He glanced up at me, then looked away.

I walked over to him. "Colin, can I talk to you?"

"Sure." He didn't look at me and continued working.

"I mean, really *talk* to you?" He kept working. "Face to face?"

He stopped and turned to me. "What do you want to talk about?"

"I want to explain some things to you. Could I buy you a Pepsi or something?"

He paused a moment, then he sighed. "Okay. I guess."

He grabbed his jacket and we left school. He led me to the student parking lot and we climbed into his beat-up Escort.

"This your car?" I asked.

"Yes." He looked over at me quickly. "You don't think it's going to get a paint job while we're drinking Pepsi, do you?"

"No. Colin, I can't tell you how sorry I am that that happened! What did your dad say?"

"Read a few bathroom walls at school, and you'll have the general idea."

"Oh, boy."

"It was the best car he'd ever owned."

He drove us to Wendy's, and I bought us Pepsis and an order of fries to share. We slid into a booth in the back corner.

"Colin, I owe you an explanation for what happened to your dad's car."

"I'm listening."

"I have to go back several weeks." I took a big breath and let it out. "You see, I was in the hills with the people who set that cabin on fire."

He frowned and watched me steadily.

"You probably won't believe me, but I tried to stop them from doing it. We knew Heath Quinn was inside—we'd seen him go in—and I pounded on the door and yelled for him to come out; I told him that the cabin was going to be set on fire." I stopped, embarrassed. "Obviously, I didn't do a very good job. I didn't get him to come out."

"How many people were with you?" Colin pulled a french fry out of the little sack and ate it.

"Five."

"Nikki and Matt. Who else?"

"Sean, Randy, and Brandi."

Colin's eyes opened wide. "Two of them are dead."

"Yes. I'm pretty sure Heath somehow survived the fire. I think he killed Sean and Matt."

"You think he painted my dad's car?"

I nodded. "I don't know who else could have done it."

I told him about how Eve and I had climbed the tree and gotten into Heath's attic. "He has articles about the fire and Sean's murder taped up all over the attic. You should see it, Colin. It's like something you'd read in the newspaper about a mass murderer."

He sat back in the booth and fingered his straw thoughtfully.

"He struck me as a very angry person even before the fire," I said.

Colin nodded. "In this town, you're either a somebody or a cipher."

"I've been trying so hard to find him," I said. "I want to talk to him and let him know that I'm an outsider, too. There are a lot of people at Franklin Heights High who don't fit in for one reason or another. We all need to stick together and help one another."

For the first time, Colin looked at me with some genuine warmth in his eyes. "Yeah," he said. "You're right." He shook his head. "Poor Heath."

"So that's what's been going on. I don't think writing an article about Heath is a good idea if he's killing people."

"I agree. Do the police know all this?"

"They do now—as of last night. They came to ask Nikki a lot of questions about Matt."

"Did they think Heath could be the murderer?"

"The detective didn't say, but he sure was listening carefully. And he took a lot of notes."

Colin leaned forward. "Are you in danger? Do you need anything?"

"No, thanks," I said. I smiled. "If you happen to see Heath, though, please let me know."

"He seems to be keeping himself pretty well hidden."

"He sure is."

A figure passed the window outside and I looked up. That dark-haired guy—the Mystery Man—hurried across the parking lot, glancing through the window at us as he rushed past. He paused at the curb, then ran across the busy street, dodging traffic in both directions.

"Colin, do you know that guy?"

"Who?"

"He just crossed the street, wearing the blue cap."

Colin peered in the direction I was pointing. "No, I don't think so. Why?"

"He's connected to Heath in some way. I saw him coming out of the Quinns' home the other day when Eve and I went there to interview Mr. Quinn. I think that guy was there uninvited."

Colin frowned. "That's strange." He looked back across the street. "I didn't get a very good look at him, but I don't think he was familiar."

"Isn't that unusual?"

"What do you mean?"

"I mean, in a town this size? Haven't you seen most of the people in town? Wouldn't you recognize someone who lives here?"

He looked surprised. "Not necessarily. Franklin Heights isn't *that* small." He touched the paper bag of french fries. "You want to finish those fries?"

I smiled. "No, I don't want any. You take them."

We slid out of the booth, and I left half my Pepsi on the table. I wasn't in the mood for eating. I was still wound up from telling Colin everything that had happened in the last couple of weeks.

I was glad I'd told him. At least he didn't seem to be as angry as he was.

We walked out to the parking lot.

"I'll give you a lift home," he said. "Thanks for the Pepsi and fries."

"Sure."

I smiled at him, and he smiled back. Good. We were friends again.

We walked toward his car.

Suddenly, he stopped and his eyes nearly bugged out of his head.

"Look!—What happened? My car! Look at my car!"

I turned quickly toward his car.

His car sat in its spot with four flat tires sagging on the pavement.

~15

Colin furiously threw his keys on the ground.

"Who did *this*?" he shouted. He began pacing back and forth behind his car. "Who did this to my car? I'll kill him! I swear I will!"

He stopped and leveled his gaze at me.

"You think Heath did this? Because I was with you? Is that what you're going to tell me, Julia?"

I shook my head. "I think the Mystery Man did it."

"Oh, great!" he said, throwing his arms up. "The Mystery Man! Well, that should make it easy to find him! We'll just tell the cops to track down the Mystery Man."

"He was just here, Colin. He passed the window and looked in and hurried off across the street! I told you, I think he's involved with Heath somehow."

"Why would he let the air out of my tires?" Colin said. "Why would he *do* that? I wasn't in the hills with you guys."

"I don't know."

"Maybe he painted my dad's car, too."

"It's possible," I said.

Colin made an exasperated noise. "Well, I'll have to get someone to come from a service station." He looked at me. "I guess you'll have to get yourself home."

"No problem. I'll walk. It isn't far."

I stooped down, picked up his keys and handed them to him.

I nearly said, at least he didn't *slash* your tires—or paint your car. But I knew that wouldn't make him feel any better. He was too angry to get any solace from that.

He walked back into Wendy's, and I headed toward Nikki's house. It was only about six blocks; I'd be there in ten minutes.

I walked along the street—there were no sidewalks in this part of the neighborhood—and I kept thinking, why would the Mystery Man have wanted to disable Colin's car? It didn't make sense.

I turned down Dalewood Avenue, my sneakers scuffling along the pavement.

That's when I first saw the van.

It was in back of me, about a half-block away, driving very slowly. That cinnamon color.

Just like the van that had followed Eve and me to Petie's that night.

My pulse quickened, and I went over the options in my mind.

One, I could run. Two, I could continue at this pace and see what happened.

I decided on the second choice. I didn't know whether I was in danger. The van was the same color, but that didn't mean it was the same van.

But even if it was the identical van, I didn't know that the driver meant to hurt me.

I suspected that the driver was the Mystery Man. He had been turning up a lot lately. He'd shown up at school right after Heath was murdered; he'd watched Nikki, Matt, Brandi, Randy, and me at the park and taken pictures of us; he'd entered Heath's house and run when I called to him; and he had probably just let the air out of Colin's tires.

Now he was following me. He hadn't done anything dangerous yet. At least, not that I knew of.

Unless he was the murderer.

Panic grabbed hold of my chest. Was it possible that Heath *wasn't* the person who had shot Sean and Matt?

I glanced back at the van. It was far enough away that I couldn't see the driver's face.

I quickened my pace. I glanced back again; the driver was staying with me, nearly a half-block behind.

What did he want? Why didn't he speed up to come and get me? Or isn't that what he wanted? Was he waiting for a more secluded street? He wouldn't have to wait long. The houses along the next street were farther apart and set farther back from the curb. Plus there was a wooded area I'd pass with no houses around it.

I still had more than four blocks before I'd get home. A lot could happen in four blocks.

I turned into an alley and started to run. Behind me, the van's engine revved loudly as it came roaring after me.

I ran as hard as I could, but the van was gaining on me.

Swerving to the right, I ran into a backyard and between two houses. There was no way the driver could follow me in the van. I glanced back to see the van roar off down the alley.

I knew what it would do. It would turn right twice and head for me as I crossed the street in front of these houses.

I couldn't outrun the van.

It was better to hide.

I ran back the way I'd come. A side door to a garage on the alley stood open. I hesitated a moment in the doorway, then walked inside. The large door was closed. There was one small window on one wall and another window in the side door that still stood open.

No car was there; there wasn't room for one. The garage was filled with power tools, a lawn mower, a wooden ladder, a snow blower, rakes, snow shovels, bags of peat, and gardening tools.

I ducked behind a large metal garden cart, making myself as small as I could.

A long silence passed. Gradually, the hammering of my heart slowed. I peeked over the cart toward the door and saw nothing.

Maybe he had driven away, I thought. Maybe he had given up trying to catch me.

At least I knew why he'd let the air out of Colin's tires.

He wanted me to walk home alone.

I straightened up and took a few steps toward the garage's side door.

A footstep outside the garage froze me in place for a moment before I scrambled back to my hiding place.

"Julia?" he said softly. "I know you're around here somewhere."

I peeked around the edge of the garden cart. The lawn mower and snow blower stood between me and the open door, but I could see part of him. He walked slowly just a few feet outside the garage.

"Julia? I know all about you and what you've been doing. You're in great danger; I hope you know that."

He paused at the door and gazed into the garage.

I didn't dare breathe. He might hear that tiny intake of air.

"In fact, if you want to stay alive, you'd better leave Franklin Heights. Go back to wherever you came from.

"If you don't"—he paused, taking a step away—"you're going to die, Julia. Just like the others who were in the hills that night."

I didn't move, didn't breathe, just closed my eyes.

Go away, I told him silently. *Go away and leave me alone.*

I wished I had psychic gifts that could *will* him away.

I waited to see what he would do next. He took a few more steps away, then walked slowly back toward the houses across the yard.

He must have parked on the street, on the other side of the homes.

Finally, I allowed myself to draw in a lungful of air.

Don't move, I told myself. He's going to be waiting for you. He'll wait in his van down the street. He knows where I'll walk to get home.

So, I decided to take another way, a long way around and approach Nikki's house from another direction. It would probably take me an extra fifteen minutes to get home.

But the Mystery Man wouldn't see me.

That was all I cared about.

"Julia, where in the world have you been?"

Aunt Helen stood in the middle of the living room, a suitcase on the floor at her feet. She looked very angry.

"This is the second time you've been out without calling us. I think we deserve a phone call if you're going to be this late coming home from school! With all the murders going on around here—"

"I'm so sorry, Aunt Helen," I said. "I should have called. I—I was delayed—my ride didn't work out."

There was no sense in telling her about the Mystery Man. She was upset enough about the murders and my living in their house.

Tears came to her eyes and her voice rose half an octave. "Jim's mother's had a stroke. We have to go to her. She's meant so much to both of us. We'll be back in a few days, I hope. Nikki called Brandi. You girls will be staying with her family until we get back."

I sighed deeply. "I'm sorry, Aunt Helen. I hope she's all right."

Aunt Helen strode to the bottom of the stairs.

"Jim? Are you ready? Julia's finally shown up." There was no mistaking the bitter edge in her voice.

"Be right down."

"I hope you'll use good judgment while we're gone," she said, turning to me.

"I will."

"And don't go out without telling Brandi's parents."

Her face looked so angry, so sad, so vulnerable all at once. I could see my mother's face in hers, and it made me feel sad for both of them. And me.

Uncle Jim hurried down the stairs carrying his own suitcase. He glanced at me but didn't speak.

"You ready?" Aunt Helen asked, her voice trembling.

"Yes. I'll load the car."

"I'm going up to say good-bye to Nikki." She disappeared up the stairs.

Now Uncle Jim turned to me.

"This is a bad time for us to leave," he said.

"We'll be all right."

"The murders—"

"Don't worry," I said. "We'll be at Brandi's house."

"Be sure they keep the doors locked."

"I will."

"If you see anything suspicious," Uncle Jim said, "don't hesitate to call the police."

"I won't."

"Better be safe than sorry."

"Don't worry, Uncle Jim," I said. "I hope your mother improves very quickly."

He glanced away and blinked watery eyes. "I hope so, too."

He walked to the stairs. "Helen?"

Aunt Helen came down. She stood in front of me with tears in her eyes. "I'm sorry for snapping at you, Julia," she said. "I just—I just . . ."

"That's okay, Aunt Helen," I said. "Have a safe trip."

She nodded and left by the back door. Uncle Jim paused at the door, then turned to me.

"Nikki said you'll be going to Brandi's in a half hour. Take care of each other, will you, Julia?"

I walked over and hugged him. "Yes, we will. Don't worry."

He nodded, embarrassed by the hug, and left.

I closed the door, locked it, and turned back to the room. It seemed so empty. So sad. So lonely.

I strolled into the kitchen.

What am I doing, I thought. I'm not hungry.

I walked around to the foyer and climbed the stairs to my room.

I didn't know it then, but this was the beginning of the longest night of my life.

~16

I stopped in front of Nikki's closed door and knocked.

"What do you want?"

"May I come in?"

I heard feet tromping across the hardwood floor. The door was yanked open.

"No. What do you want?"

I leaned on the door frame. "I just wanted to say hi. I'm sorry about your grandmother."

"I hate her."

I let that pass. "When is Brandi's family expecting us?"

"They're not."

"I thought we were going to—"

"We're not going anywhere," she snapped. "I just said that to get my parents off my back."

I sighed. "You hungry? I could make us a pizza. Or we could order one to be delivered."

"Get a delivered one."

She closed the door in my face.

"What kind?" I asked.

"Onion and cheese," she said from behind the door.

I ordered it from the phone in Aunt Helen's room. Then I went into my room and sat in a chair next to the front window.

It was still light outside, but the sun was sinking lower in the sky. Long shadows were cast across the lawn and into the street.

I didn't feel like doing homework. I didn't even feel like watching TV or eating pizza.

I got up and paced around the house, and I checked to see that the windows and doors were locked on both floors.

The doorbell rang. I checked through the window and saw a guy in a Pizza Hut delivery cap.

I paid for the pizza, locked the door again, and called Nikki to come downstairs.

We ate at the kitchen table while the darkness grew outside.

"What are you going to do tonight?" I asked her.

"I don't know." She didn't look at me.

"Homework?"

"I don't have any."

"You want to watch a movie? I saw Uncle Jim's collection downstairs. I'd like to see a comedy—"

"Whatever I'm doing, I'm not doing it with you."

I put down the slice of pizza in my hand. "Nikki, are you still angry that I told the detective what's been going on?"

"What do you think?"

"Matt's dead," I said.

"Well, *I'm* not," she said.

"That's right, but you will be if you don't help the police find the murderer."

Nikki's eyes filled up with tears. "I can't believe he's dead. Are you coming to the funeral on Friday?"

"Of course. Nikki, I know how much you cared about Matt."

She sniffed and blew her nose on her napkin. "I miss him so much."

"That's why we should help the police in any way we can. We should help them find Matt's and Sean's murderer."

She nodded and sighed. "I guess." She stared at her plate. "I don't want any more."

"I'm not very hungry, either. I'll wrap it and put it in the fridge."

I flipped on the kitchen light. She sat quietly at the table while I cleaned up.

"You feel like playing Monopoly or Trivial Pursuit or something?" I asked her.

"No. But I guess I'll watch a movie if it isn't sad."

"Okay. I'll go downstairs and pick out a couple of funny ones."

I ran down the basement stairs and pulled out *National Lampoon's Vacation* and *National Lampoon's Christmas Vacation*. I'd seen them both, and they were guaranteed to provoke laughter from people in the saddest moods.

I climbed back upstairs and walked into the living room.

The phone rang.

"Hello?" Nikki had answered it in the kitchen. "Julia, it's for you."

I set the tapes down on the TV and walked back into the kitchen where I took the receiver from Nikki.

"Hello?"

"Julia?" It was a guy's voice, muffled so that it was unrecognizable.

"Yes?"

"Hi, Julia. I'm watching you."

"Who's this?"

"The Watcher."

"What?"

"You're wearing that blue sweater that makes you look so sexy."

"What do you want?"

"Just wanted you to know I'm watching you. I can see everything you do."

I hung up.

"Who was that?"

"Some jerk." My heart was beating hard, but I kept my voice under control. "Come on, let's watch the movie."

We went into the living room.

The phone rang again.

"Don't answer it," I said.

"But Matt's mom was going to call me about the funeral. I'm supposed to go to their house afterward and—"

The phone rang again.

"Okay. But if it's that jerk, hang up."

Nikki ran into the kitchen, and I followed. "Hello?"

I watched her face. At first, there was no expression. Then her eyes got wide.

"How do you know that?" She frowned. "What do you mean?"

A crash behind me in the dining room sent my heart into my throat. Nikki screamed and dropped the phone.

I whirled around to see that a window was broken. Shards of glass glittered on the hardwood floor. A round package lay next to a potted plant in the corner.

"He said he had a message for us!" Nikki cried.

"Hang up the phone," I said.

She did.

I walked to the package that had crashed through the dining room window and picked it up. It was a rock wrapped in paper and tied with a string.

I took the paper from the rock and looked at it.

Written on that old typewriter were two words that set my heart thundering against my ribs:

YOU'RE NEXT!

17

The phone rang again. I stared at it. I didn't know whether to pick it up or not. If I kept him talking, maybe I could figure out what to do.

"Don't answer it!" Nikki said, backing away as if the telephone itself were the killer.

"I think I should talk to him."

"Don't!"

The phone rang shrilly, insistently.

I picked up the receiver. "Hello?"

"Hello, Julia."

"You're right outside the house, aren't you?"

"How'd you guess?"

"On a cellular phone."

"Wave to me, Julia. I can see you through the window. You look pretty tonight."

I covered the mouthpiece and whispered to Nikki, "Close the shutters!"

She did, and he laughed softly. "You think those shutters can keep me out? You're wrong. I can get in anytime I want."

"Leave us alone."

"Oh, but this is so much fun. I like watching

people squirm. Matt's a good squirmer. He squirmed plenty just before I killed him. Sean didn't even see it coming. That wasn't as much fun."

"Is this Heath?"

"You got it."

"How did you survive the fire?"

"What does it matter? Maybe I flew out the window."

"No one wanted you to die, Heath. Why would we want to kill you? We don't even know you!"

"You don't have to know someone to hate them."

"We don't hate you."

"I think you do. Matt did. He and Nikki and all of their friends hate me."

"No, they don't. I wish you could understand that."

"They killed me because I was different. I wasn't an athlete like Matt and Sean and Randy. I wasn't anybody special."

I stopped short. "You aren't Heath, are you?"

There was a pause. "Why do you say that?"

"You're talking about yourself in the past tense."

He laughed. "I'm back from the dead, didn't you know that, Julia? I'm here to avenge my death."

"What's he saying?" Nikki whispered.

I shook my head at Nikki.

"Tell Nikki that tonight she will die."

"I will not."

He laughed again. "I guess she'll just have to find that out for herself."

I had to get help, and the only way was over the phone. We certainly couldn't run out into the night.

If I hung up, would the line disconnect? If not, he could keep the line tied up so I wouldn't be able to phone the police.

The only way I'd know was to try.

I hung up, and before I could pick it up again, the phone rang.

"What did he say?" Nikki said.

I stared at the phone.

"He couldn't have dialed that fast." Even with a fast redial button, he couldn't have made the call that quickly.

"What did he say?"

"I'll tell you in a minute." I picked it up. "Hello?"

"Julia, this is Eve."

"Oh, Eve! I need to have the line clear to call the police."

"What's wrong?"

"Somebody's outside the house, calling and threatening us."

She gasped. "It must be Heath!"

"I don't know for sure. But I have to hang up and call for help."

"Okay, I'll hang up. And don't worry. Help will come soon. Call me back after the police get there."

"I will. Bye."

I hung up, waited a moment, then lifted the phone and dialed 911.

I could hear it ringing.

Then it stopped.

"Hello?" I said startled.

No, don't let the line be dead, I thought.

"Hello?" I flicked the button up and down.

I looked over at Nikki, who was watching me with a pale face.

"He cut the telephone line, didn't he?" she said softly.

"Looks that way." I hung up.

Nikki started breathing hard. "What are we going to do?"

"We have to keep everything locked up," I said. "Maybe Eve will call the police for us."

"But I heard you tell her that *you* were going to call 911."

"I know, but she'll expect a call back from me after the police would've arrived. When I don't call, maybe she'll call the police."

Nikki was standing about ten feet from me. Even from that distance, I could see her trembling.

"But that could take *hours!*"

"We'll just have to hold on. Maybe she'll be curious about what's going on and call back."

"But she'll get a dead line!" Nikki's eyes were wild.

"And then she'll call the police."

"Maybe," she said. "And maybe we'll be dead by then. Well, I'm not going to let him kill *me!*"

Nikki ran to the basement door, threw it open, and headed downstairs.

The rifle was downstairs, but Uncle Jim had locked it up.

I ran to the top of the stairs.

"What are you doing?"

The sound of breaking glass shattered the brief silence.

"Nikki!"

There was no answer.

I started down the stairs and stopped halfway when I saw Nikki walking toward me holding Uncle Jim's rifle.

"What are you doing?"

"I broke into my dad's gun cabinet." She hurried past me on the stairs. "I only found three bullets."

"Nikki, do you know how to use that?"

I followed her up to the main floor.

"What do you mean?" She walked through the living room and headed up the steps.

"Where are you going?"

"Upstairs. I'll pick him off from the window like a fish in a barrel."

I hurried after her. "Have you ever had target practice with that gun?"

"Julia, you don't have to be a rocket scientist to shoot a gun. You load it, aim, and fire. I've watched my dad load it. It's not hard."

"You can't shoot someone for threatening you over the phone," I said.

"Watch me."

"Nikki! Wait, we need to talk about this."

I followed her into my bedroom. She flipped on the light, set the rifle on my bed, and fished the bullets out of her pocket.

"That's been your solution from the beginning,"

Nikki said. "Talk, talk, talk. And look where we are. Sean and Matt are both dead, and Heath is outside planning a way to get in here and murder us. So I'm not talking with you or with him. I'm going to stop him once and for all. Permanently."

She sat on my bed and slid the bullets into the gun. Then she threw a lever down on the side of the gun and pulled it back.

"Now it's ready."

Nikki was right about one thing. We needed protection. I knew that Heath—or whoever was on the phone—planned to kill us. But if Nikki couldn't shoot straight—or worse, if she panicked and shot at anything that moved, including her foot or my head—we were in big trouble.

"Nikki, I've done some target shooting with my dad," I said. "Would you give it to me?"

"No way. You'd never use it."

"I would if I had to. I promise I would."

"No way."

She got up and turned out the light, then walked to the window and looked out. I stood beside her and searched the front yard below for a moving figure.

I saw no one.

But I did see something else.

A *van*. It was parked at the curb across the street under the light.

"The Mystery Man!" I whispered.

"The who?"

"It's the Mystery Man. The guy we saw at school and then at the park. He took pictures of us, remember?"

"That's who's outside?"

"It must be. That's his van. I've seen it a couple of times."

"It's not Heath?"

"I don't think so."

"What would this Mystery Man have against us?"

"I don't know."

"Well, I'm ready for him," Nikki said.

We sat at the window and stared out into the yard. If only this street weren't so deserted, I thought. We could scream for help and the neighbors would call the police.

A dark figure moved from the shadows behind a tall pine and walked directly up our sidewalk.

"That's him!" Nikki said. She stood up and pulled the window up a few inches.

"You're not going to shoot him!" I said.

Ding-dong.

Nikki looked at me. "He rang the doorbell? Does he think we're complete morons?"

It was baffling. When you're besieged in your own house, you don't expect the killer to politely ring the doorbell.

Nikki pushed up the glass in the combination window and looked down below.

"I can't see him. He's too close to the house."

"Julia!" a voice called from below.

"Who's that?" Nikki asked.

"I don't know." I stood up and looked out the window.

"Who is it?" I called.

"I tried to call, but the line was dead."

"The phone wires have been cut to the house," I said. "Who are you?"

"You don't know me, but I'm a friend."

The Mystery Man, a friend? He followed me in his van and told me I was going to die. Right.

"If you're a friend, call the police," I said.

"I want to talk to you. I can help."

"If you want to help," I repeated, "call the police."

Silence.

"Hello?" I said.

There was no answer.

"The Mystery Man was the guy on the phone, right?" Nikki said.

"I think so."

"Then he cut the phone wires, and now he says he wants to help?"

"It doesn't make sense," I said.

"Is Heath out there, too?"

"I don't know who's out there," I said. "I just know that we can't trust anybody right now."

"So what do we do?"

"We wait," I said. "Eve will call the police eventually. At least, I hope she will."

~18

We sat at the window for at least half an hour without hearing or seeing anyone.

"I wish he'd just get it over with," Nikki said. "Show himself or try something so I can get a good aim at him. I'll show him what happens when he kills my friends. He'll get it right back."

Another thirty minutes dragged by. I couldn't understand why Eve hadn't sent the police by now. Hadn't she tried to call us back since the lines were cut?

"I have to pee," Nikki said. She got up, leaving the gun on the floor, and walked out of the room.

I picked up the gun and slid it under the bed.

I knew where it was if I needed it, but Nikki wouldn't be able to blow off her head—or mine—if she panicked.

Maybe I was crazy, but I still thought I might be able to talk to the murderer, whoever he was, and convince him to stop the killing. Didn't he let me get away from the park that day? He could have shot me then, but he didn't. The people who he'd shot were involved in the fire in the hills. Maybe he would spare me, and I could perhaps talk him into leaving Nikki and the others alone.

A loud crash came from downstairs.

Nikki charged back into the room.

"What was that?" she gasped.

She scrambled to the window. *"Where is it?"* she screamed. *"Where's the rifle?"*

"Forget the rifle, Nikki," I said. "I'm afraid you'll blow somebody's head off."

"Tell me where it is!" she screamed. She lurched at me and smacked me hard in the face.

I pushed her away. She ran to the corner of the room, sobbing, and curled up in a ball on the floor. "We'll be killed, we'll be killed," she cried.

"Please stay here," I said.

I listened at the bedroom door and heard nothing.

I quietly opened the door and peeked out.

"Where are you going?" Nikki whispered anxiously.

"I'll be back."

I slipped out the door and softly closed the door behind me. Tiptoeing into the hall I listened for noise from downstairs. The Mystery Man must be down there, listening, too, in the dark.

After several minutes at the top of the steps and hearing nothing, I started slowly and carefully down the stairs. Halfway down, I spotted the broken-out window in the living room. Most of the glass had been cleared from the frame. In the diffuse light that filtered in from the kitchen, I could see the shards of glass glistening on the floor.

"Hello," I said. "I know you're in here. I want to talk to you."

One by one, I took the remaining stairs down, looking back and forth across the living room, trying to see him.

"I just want to talk. Will you show me where you are?"

There was no answer.

At the bottom of the stairs, I stopped. That's when I spotted him.

A dark figure standing in deep shadows at the far corner of the living room.

"Please talk to me," I said.

An explosion rocked the house and blew out a window next to the Mystery Man.

I whirled around to see Nikki behind me on the stairs, holding the rifle.

"Nikki!" I cried. "Put that down!"

I lunged for it, but she darted backward up the stairs, still clutching it to her.

Footsteps rushed past, and when I looked back at the corner, the Mystery Man was gone.

I knew he now thought we meant to kill him. I wouldn't be able to convince him to talk to me after Nikki had shot at him.

Now it was time to arm myself. I ran to the kitchen and pulled a long knife out of the drawer. I meant to use it only in self-defense. I realized that it would be of little use if he had a gun—since that's the way both Sean and Matt had been killed—but it was all I had. If I had the chance, I'd try and get the rifle away from Nikki.

Clutching the knife tightly, I walked into the dining room. The shrubs stirred in the breeze outside the broken-out window.

It occurred to me that I could run outside right now and get away, but Nikki was upstairs. I couldn't leave her alone to go and get help, even though she had the rifle.

I peered around the wall of the dining room into the short hall beside the stairs. No one was there.

I walked slowly across the hall and toward the front door.

Another explosion nearly knocked me off my feet and ripped a hole in the door a foot from my nose.

Nikki shrieked from the stairs.

"Julia, it's you!"

"Nikki!" I screamed. *"You could have killed me!"*

I charged up the stairs after her and caught hold of her foot on the top step. I wrestled with her and tried to pry the gun out of her hands. The rifle went off again with a *boom!*

We stopped struggling. That was the third shot, the end of the bullets.

Nikki's eyes grew wide with horror.

"Look what you made me do," she cried. "Now there aren't any bullets left!"

She shoved the rifle away from her on the floor and ran into her bedroom.

I followed after her. She crouched in her closet, crying, and closed the door.

What were we going to do now? The rifle was useless. And the knife . . .

Where was the knife?

"Oh, no!" I said.

"What?" came a muffled sob from inside the closet.

"I had a knife, but I dropped it when you shot at me."

"I didn't know it was you!"

I thought I heard a footstep on the stairs. I moved quickly and locked the bedroom door.

"Where is he?"

"I think he might be on his way up the stairs," I whispered. I looked over at her window. "Nikki, we have to get out of here."

"He's coming to get us."

"Come out of the closet."

I raised the window.

"What are you doing?" she whispered, poking her head out of the closet.

"We're going out this way. Come here, quickly."

The doorknob rattled, and Nikki scrambled to my side.

"He's here! He's at the door! Hurry!"

I pulled the glass out of the combination window and then the screen.

"You go first," I whispered.

I helped her climb out of the window and onto the flat garage roof.

I threw one leg over the window sill.

An explosion rocked the house and the bedroom door crashed open.

Without waiting another second, I pulled myself outside onto the roof.

In a moment, a dark face appeared at the window right behind me.

"Hold it," he said. "Don't move."

Nikki whimpered while he climbed out the window. He turned and faced us.

I peered at him in the dark. "Heath?"

"Yeah."

Was it really Heath? I took a step closer and gasped.

"*Colin!* What are doing here? What's going on?"

"I fooled you, didn't I?" he said, pointing his gun at me. "Heath and I are built the same, and with my hair greased back, we look a lot alike."

"You mean, it was you all along? *You* wrote those notes and . . . and you killed Sean and Matt?"

"They deserved to die," he said. "They killed my half-brother."

"Your half-brother? Heath?"

"He was my dad's son. Dad was married to Heath's mother for less than a year. They were divorced, and soon after that, Heath was born. Then his mother remarried Mr. Quinn, who's a terrible alcoholic."

Colin shook his head. "I always knew I should look out for Heath since he was my brother. But I wasn't very popular, myself. Getting good grades counts against you in this town.

"So I stood by while the popular kids treated him bad. I watched while they laughed at him, beat him up, and pushed his face in the dirt.

"I even joined in to taunt him sometimes. I mocked Heath—not many people knew we were brothers—and I limped around the playground. I hated myself for doing it, but I did it anyway. I didn't want to be made fun of, so I helped the others make fun of Heath—my own brother.''

"You were just a kid," I said.

"I knew better," he said, a bitter edge in his voice. "It wasn't that long ago.

"But I couldn't let them murder him and get off without punishment. I owed that to Heath. So I finally stood up for him. I should've done that when he was alive."

"But, Colin, killing the people who were on the hill that night won't bring Heath back."

"It doesn't matter. He would've wanted me to do this. I bought a jacket like the one Heath always wore and asked myself what would he do if he had survived. I know you didn't set fire to the cabin. Neither did Nikki, although she loved every minute of it."

"No, Colin," Nikki cried. "I swear. I tried to get them to stop. Honest."

"You're a liar, Nikki," Colin said. "I heard you and Matt talking to Julia in the cafeteria one day. I was standing right around the doorway from you and heard every word. You were talking to Julia about writing that article. That's when I realized that all of you were involved.

"I'd thought writing an article about the outsiders around school was great," he said to me. "I thought maybe people might finally treat Heath differently. Then he disappeared, and I found out you were involved in the fire."

"So Heath died in the fire?" I said.

"You all killed him."

"What about his attic? Eve and I found—"

"I'd already left that receipt in Heath's room in case Mr. Quinn took you up there during your interview. Then when you told me you were going to stake out his house, I got the idea to lead you inside. I knew you were watching me. I set up the attic to look as if he were staying there. It was easy. Mr. Quinn is drunk a lot and doesn't hear much. After I figured out how to get in using the tree, I usually left through the house."

"You even put the typewriter in the attic."

"All the notes were written on it." Colin sounded proud of his work.

"Was that you in the concession stand at the park?" I asked. "Did you point a gun at me?"

"I nearly shot you, too. But I still wasn't sure how you fit into this whole story. So I decided to wait. I asked you to the movie so I could talk to you about Nikki. You said you were getting along with her, so I figured you didn't hate her for what she and her friends had done to Heath."

"What about the paint on your father's Volvo?"

In the dim light, I saw Colin grin. "My dad couldn't afford a car like that. I stole it. Then I paid that kid at the theater to paint it later while we were having pizza. I left the car unlocked, and the paint was in the trunk. All he had to do was spray the words on it."

"You hired a little boy—?"

"I called him and told him to meet me at the movie theater on that Saturday night for instructions."

I stared at him. "I can't believe all the trouble

you went to to make us think Heath was still alive."

"Heath would've liked it. I finally did something for him."

"You even came to my window," Nikki said, "right out here on the roof."

Colin grinned. "You scream loud, Nikki. I've been looking forward to hearing it again." He brought up his hand and pointed the gun at Nikki.

She screamed.

"Very good," he said. "But louder next time."

Nikki whimpered and took a step back.

"Dive," he said. "Off the roof. Go on."

"Don't do this, please, Colin," I begged.

I edged a little closer to Colin.

"Do it!" Colin ordered Nikki. "You murdering witch! Dive head first!"

A noise at the window startled me. "Julia! Are you all right?"

I didn't know who it was—I didn't care. When Colin turned to see who it was, I lunged at him to grab the gun away.

He dropped the gun, lost his balance, and stumbled backward. He cried out and fell head first off the edge of the roof.

I heard his body hit the ground. Then there was an awful silence.

~19

"Who *are* you?" I asked.

Nikki paced in the side yard, while I sat on the ground next to Colin and waited for the police and the ambulance. Every few seconds Nikki looked up the street to see if they were coming. The Mystery Man leaned against the garage, watching us, and rubbed the back of his head.

Colin was alive, but just barely. He was very badly injured, though, so we didn't dare move him. I held his hand, but I'm sure he wasn't aware of it.

"I thought you were the killer for a while," I said.

The Mystery Man frowned. "Me? I was trying to find out who killed Heath."

"You have a name?" Nikki asked.

"Rick Lenhart."

"Lenhart?" I said.

"I'm Eve's brother. I was Heath's physical therapist. He'd been seeing me for about a year; we were working on his leg, trying to gain some strength in it and get rid of that limp. He'd injured it years earlier in a car accident. Heath and I'd gotten to be good friends."

"Did Eve know all along that you were looking for Heath's killer?"

"She didn't even know I *knew* Heath until she saw me at the Quinn house that day you two came to interview Heath's dad."

"Why did she pretend not to know you—and why did you run away?"

"I'd been very distracted after Heath was thought to be dead. She thought I was in some kind of trouble. She also thought I'd broken into the Quinn house, when I'd really just found the door unlocked—as you had. I ran because I was afraid you'd think I'd had something to do with Heath's death."

He smiled. "Then you confessed to her about being in the hills the night of the fire."

"She *told* you about that?"

"She wanted me to know that you were innocent," Rick said. "I'd seen you all talking in the cafeteria and overheard a couple of words. I thought you were involved, somehow. Eve wanted me to know the truth." He paused. "Looking back on it, I remember seeing Colin standing near the cafeteria door that day getting money out of his pocket. I didn't know who he was and assumed he was pulling out lunch money. He must have been listening to you."

"You followed us to Petie's, didn't you?" I asked.

"Yes. Eve told me you were going out to ask the clerk if he recognized Heath's picture. I was concerned about her going out so late with a killer on the loose." He laughed softly. "She read me the riot act when she got home."

I felt a need to tie up all the loose ends.

"So she didn't tell you about our stakeout?"

"What stakeout?"

"That's what I thought. Did you follow Colin and me to Wendy's this afternoon?"

Could it have only been this afternoon? That memory seemed a week old.

Rick nodded. "This morning I went back over Heath's file and read about his family. When I saw that he had a half-brother who went to Franklin Heights High, it started coming together for me. I wanted to get you away from him, so I let the air out of Colin's tires and came after you. I didn't mean to scare you. I just wanted to warn you that you were in danger."

He paused, gazing at me. "Eve really likes you, you know. She was worried about you. She said you'd gotten dragged into this and were in danger. After she talked to you on the phone tonight, she asked me to come over and see if you were all right. Actually, she wanted to come, too, but I wouldn't let her."

He grimaced and rubbed his head again.

"Are you okay?" I asked him.

"Headache. Colin hit me on the back of the head with something."

"Were you talking to me at the window when you were hit?"

"Yes, I think so. It must've knocked me out."

Sirens sounded faintly in the distance.

"They're coming," Nikki said.

"I'm sorry you were hurt," I said to Rick, "but I'm very glad you came here tonight. Your timing was perfect. If you hadn't appeared at the window when you did—" I shook my head. "I don't want to think about it."

"I'm glad I got here in time, too," Rick said. "Eve will be very relieved. She's waiting for me to call."

"She's going to be shocked when she finds out it was Colin who was behind all of the notes and the killing. She really liked him."

"I know," Rick said. "She needs some lessons in character judgment." He smiled. "She was right about you, though."

The sirens grew louder and louder. Two police cars screeched to a stop at the curb. An ambulance followed close behind them.

"It's over," Rick murmured, staring off at the whirling red lights. "The killing is finally over."

20

"I'm sorry I didn't tell you about Rick," Eve said, kicking a stone on the sidewalk leading to the school.

I'd called her last night from a neighbor's house after the ambulance had taken Colin to the hospital and after Detective Harley had asked Nikki and Rick and me a hundred questions each. She and I had agreed to meet early before school the next day.

"I didn't want you to be angry that I told him," she said. "There aren't a lot of people at school who I feel close to, and I didn't want you to hate me."

"That's okay," I said.

"Colin sure did fool me," Eve said. "And to think while I was drooling over him, he was out on a killing spree."

"People can surprise you."

"What about Nikki and Brandi and Randy?" she asked. "What will happen to them?"

"Detective Harley told me he thought the court would go pretty easy on them. None of them set the fire, and they hadn't been in trouble before that night in the hills. Besides, their intent wasn't to kill him. I'm not going to be charged as an accessory because Nikki, Brandi, and Randy all told him that I tried to stop Matt from setting the fire." I sighed. "So, as your brother said, it's over. The killing is over. Thank goodness."

"Now you can relax," Eve said, "and enjoy the semester. There really are some nice people here."

I smiled. "That sounds good to me."

I looked up at the school building. For the first time, it seemed like a friendly, inviting place.

Might as well give it another chance, I thought. What did I have to lose?

Eve and I headed up the steps and into the school.

TERRIFYING TALES OF SPINE-TINGLING SUSPENSE

THE MAN WHO WAS POE Avi
71192-3/ $3.99 US/ $4.99 Can

DYING TO KNOW Jeff Hammer
76143-2/ $3.50 US/ $4.50 Can

NIGHT CRIES Barbara Steiner
76990-5/ $3.50 US/ $4.25 Can

CHAIN LETTER Christopher Pike
89968-X/ $3.99 US/ $4.99 Can

THE EXECUTIONER Jay Bennett
79160-9/ $3.99 US/ $4.99 Can

THE LAST LULLABY Jesse Osburn
77317-1/ $3.99 US/ $4.99 Can

THE DREAMSTALKER Barbara Steiner
76611-6/ $3.50 US/ $4.25 Can

Buy these books at your local bookstore or use this coupon for ordering:

Mail to: Avon Books, Dept BP, Box 767, Rte 2, Dresden, TN 38225   D
Please send me the book(s) I have checked above.
❏ My check or money order—no cash or CODs please—for $_____ is enclosed (please add $1.50 to cover postage and handling for each book ordered—Canadian residents add 7% GST).
❏ Charge my VISA/MC Acct#_____ Exp Date_____
Minimum credit card order is two books or $7.50 (please add postage and handling charge of $1.50 per book—Canadian residents add 7% GST). For faster service, call 1-800-762-0779. Residents of Tennessee, please call 1-800-633-1607. Prices and numbers are subject to change without notice. Please allow six to eight weeks for delivery.

Name_____
Address_____
City_____ State/Zip_____
Telephone No._____   THO 0595

SPINE-TINGLING SUSPENSE FROM AVON FLARE

NICOLE DAVIDSON

THE STALKER	76645-0/ $3.50 US/ $4.50 Can
CRASH COURSE	75964-0/ $3.99 US/ $4.99 Can
WINTERKILL	75965-9/ $3.99 US/ $4.99 Can
DEMON'S BEACH	76644-2/ $3.50 US/ $4.25 Can
FAN MAIL	76995-6/ $3.50 US/ $4.50 Can
SURPRISE PARTY	76996-4/ $3.50 US/ $4.50 Can
NIGHT TERRORS	72243-7/ $3.99 US/ $4.99 Can

THE BAND
by Carmen Adams — 77328-7/ $3.99 US/ $4.99 Can

SHOW ME THE EVIDENCE
by Alane Ferguson — 70962-7/ $3.99 US/ $4.99 Can

EVIL IN THE ATTIC
by Linda Piazza — 77576-X/ $3.99 US/ $4.99 Can

RATS IN THE ATTIC AND OTHER STORIES TO MAKE YOUR SKIN CRAWL
by G.E. Stanley — 77389-9/ $3.99 US/ $4.99 Can

Buy these books at your local bookstore or use this coupon for ordering:

Mail to: Avon Books, Dept BP, Box 767, Rte 2, Dresden, TN 38225   D
Please send me the book(s) I have checked above.
❑ My check or money order—no cash or CODs please—for $_____ is enclosed (please add $1.50 to cover postage and handling for each book ordered—Canadian residents add 7% GST).
❑ Charge my VISA/MC Acct#_____ Exp Date_____
Minimum credit card order is two books or $7.50 (please add postage and handling charge of $1.50 per book—Canadian residents add 7% GST). For faster service, call 1-800-762-0779. Residents of Tennessee, please call 1-800-633-1607. Prices and numbers are subject to change without notice. Please allow six to eight weeks for delivery.

Name_____
Address_____
City_____ State/Zip_____
Telephone No._____   YAH 0595